Laura was intrigued by the beautiful box

She had coveted it since first seeing it in the antique-store window. She was so lost in her thoughts that she did not notice the tall man approaching her. "Beautiful, isn't it?" She spun round wide-eyed to find Tom Farrell staring down at her.

"I...I beg your pardon?" she faltered.

"The silver casket," he said softly.

"Oh, yes," she sighed. "It's lovely."

"Do you want it?" he asked expressionlessly. Her head jerked toward him.

"Yes, I want it," she answered. "And if you'll excuse me, Mr. Farrell...." She had to get away, but before she could move he reached out and held her. He felt the tremor that ran through her at his touch. "If I've offended you," he said gently, "I'm sorry. Will you have dinner with me tonight?"

Her heart leaped at his invitation. Then she remembered his wife. "No, thank you, Mr. Farrell," she said stiltedly. This man, her instincts told her, had the power to destroy her.

PATRICIA LAKE

the silver casket

Harlequin Books

TORONTO • NEW YORK • LOS ANGELES • LONDON
AMSTERDAM • PARIS • SYDNEY • HAMBURG
STOCKHOLM • ATHENS • TOKYO • MILAN

Harlequin Presents first edition March 1983
ISBN 0-373-10578-9

Original hardcover edition published in 1982
by Mills & Boon Limited

CHAPTER ONE

LAURA looked at her wristwatch. One thirty-two. Grace was over half an hour late. She sighed and ordered another drink from a passing waiter, wondering what could have happened to her friend. Grace was usually extremely punctual.

Her eyes wandered around the room as she absently sipped her sherry. The restaurant was almost full with lunchtime trade, pale-faced businessmen in dark suits, talking earnestly, drinking heavily, over-elegant women in smart, beautifully-cut clothes and perfect make-up, hard-eyed and smiling, laughing so prettily.

Laura watched them all carefully, her violet eyes observing every detail, every expressive movement of jewelled hands, every red face and lazy cigar, automatically storing away the images in her mind, in case she ever needed them for her illustrations. She looked towards the door—still no sign of Grace—and her glance fell on a couple seated behind her to her left.

The woman was perfectly beautiful, tanned and fashionably slender, wearing a dark red suit that instead of clashing horridly as it should have done, somehow enhanced the auburn brilliance of her hair. But it was the man who drew Laura's eyes. He was smiling at his companion, his beautifully-moulded mouth, warm, sensual, lazy. Laura stared at that mouth, for some reason unable to drag her eyes away from the strong masculine curve of it, and for one crazy moment she could imagine it against her own, promising pleasure, promising expertise. She mentally shook herself, sternly halting her thoughts, amazed by them, but her eyes did not leave him. He was the only man in the restaurant not wearing a suit, she realised, but his casual expensively-cut clothes had a careless elegance, a style that seemed to make the other men in the room appear stuffy, overdressed and boringly conventional. There was a graceful, easy self-confidence in the way he shrugged his powerful shoulders in reply to something his companion said. Laura found herself totally absorbed in her study of him, totally unaware that she was staring, caught shock-still by his attraction, his potent masculinity, his fierce sexuality. People came to his table to talk, smiling, nodding as they passed.

Who was he? she wondered. The man's thick dark hair gleamed in the discreet overhead light as he lifted his head to greet people, to talk. His face was hard, forceful, with a lean angularity, a smooth magnetic charm in its strong lines.

As though sensing her gaze he turned his head towards her suddenly and their eyes met. Laura's heart seemed to stop beating altogether for a second as she stared into his cool, narrowed grey eyes. She felt embarrassed, very self-aware, but she could not break the contact. The grey depths were unreadable, shrewdly intelligent, and a faint smile curved his mouth as they looked at each other.

Summoning the last shreds of her willpower, her face brightly flushed, Laura finally tore her eyes away and turned from him, wondering at the tightness in her chest, the difficulty she was having in breathing normally. She had never looked at a total stranger and felt like that before.

It was a great relief to see Grace hurriedly arriving at the table, seconds later. Laura lifted her golden head and managed a smile. The man was still looking at her, she could feel those grey eyes boring into her back as surely as if he was touching her and it was difficult to smile, even at Grace, her best friend.

'You're. . . .'

'I know.' Grace did not give her a chance to finish. 'I can't believe how long it takes! The solicitors were *so* slow, I felt like screaming, and I had to ring Kate and check on the children, I felt so insecure after leaving the solicitor's office, and the traffic—I'm sorry.' She was breathless, worried, her eyes red and swollen.

Laura flashed her a sweet, sympathetic smile. 'It doesn't matter, honestly. I've been watching everybody while I waited. Very, *very* interesting. What will you have to drink?'

'Something strong,' Grace replied with dry emphasis. 'Scotch and soda, I think.'

Laura raised her eyebrows. Grace never drank at lunchtime. 'Was it as bad as that?' she asked gently.

'Worse.' Her friend's voice was husky, revealing.

Laura ordered Grace's Scotch and soda, frowning with concern.

'Do you want to tell me about it?'

'I don't think I can at the moment, not without breaking down and making a complete fool of myself.' Even as she spoke, Grace's voice broke weakly.

Laura touched her friend's hand reassuringly. 'Well, if you do need someone to talk to, you know where to come—any time.'

Grace dabbed her eyes and blew her nose, making a visible effort to pull herself together. 'Thanks, love. And I am sorry about all this. . . .'

'No need. Shall we order, or has your appetite deserted you?' Mine certainly has, she thought silently, wondering if the grey-eyed man was still behind her.

'I couldn't eat a thing,' Grace admitted. 'It's *so* ridiculous! I know better than anybody that the marriage is over—I *want* this divorce, so why am I so upset, dammit?' Laura shook her head, not knowing what to say, but wishing that there was some way to comfort her friend. Grace smiled. 'You must have something to eat, though, you mustn't let me put you off.'

'I'm not in the least bit hungry—probably that enormous breakfast I had,' Laura lied, longing to turn her head just a little bit, to see if the dark man was still in the restaurant.

'So that makes two of us. Shall I order some more drinks? We could stay here all afternoon, end up roaring drunk,' Grace laughed.

'You might as well, while the going's good. They'll probably throw us out when they realise that we're not going to be ordering any food,' Laura replied, laughing too. She felt strange. She was worried about Grace, who, although she was trying to hide it, was upset and very much on edge. And she was worried about her own reaction to the dark stranger behind her. Just to look at him had affected her deeply—and that had never happened before. It frightened her a little, somehow threatening the cosy quiet world she had created for herself. She would never see him again. She should have been relieved at that, but she wasn't. Instead she felt a vague inexplicable ache in her chest. Stupid, she admonished herself fiercely, probably the effect of all this sherry on an empty stomach. But whatever she told herself, that slight disturbing feeling lingered on as she chatted idly to Grace and sipped her third sherry of the afternoon.

She was rummaging in her handbag, searching for her cigarettes, and did not notice the long shadow that fell across her, until she looked up again, her heart leaping into her throat as she saw who stood at their table.

He was smiling at Grace, his grey eyes warm and amused. 'Hello, Grace, how have you been?' His voice was low and cool and sent a tiny shiver of awareness down Laura's spine.

'Tom! How lovely to see you—I had no idea you were back.' To Laura's amazement Grace obviously recognised him, greeting him with pleasure, as an old friend.

The man, Tom, she had called him, took both of Grace's hands in his. 'It's good to see you,' he replied smilingly. 'I was beginning to think you were ignoring me.' His eyes flicked eloquently towards the table where he and the beautiful auburn-haired woman, who now stood beside him, visibly impatient, had been sitting.

Grace clapped her hand to her forehead in dismay. 'I didn't see you!' she exclaimed in horror. 'I was dreadfully late and not in a very good mood, I'm afraid.'

'It really doesn't matter,' he laughed, shaking his dark head with wry amusement and faint mockery. Laura listened as they exchanged pleasantries, unable to stop herself staring up at him. He was well over six feet tall, his body lean and muscular with a smooth sleek grace that reminded her of some sort of big silent and dangerous cat—a panther maybe.

She felt that same disturbing weakness, stronger now it seemed, with his nearness. She could have reached out and touched him, he was so close. Her breath caught sharply as he suddenly turned to look at her, his grey eyes narrowed, unsmiling, very serious, and she lowered her head immediately, cursing the hot colour that ran over her face.

Grace was making introductions. 'Tom, this is Laura Drake, my friend and workmate. Laura, Tom Farrell.' She had to look at him again as he took her hand. His touch shivered through her, his fingers long and hard, giving the impression of leashed strength as they closed, surprisingly gently, over hers.

'Miss Drake,' he murmured in acknowledgement, his faint smile belied by the intent expression in his eyes as they rested on her uptilted face.

'How do you do Mr Farrell.' Her voice was soft, shy, her smile unknowingly breathtaking. He released her hand and, still blushing furiously, Laura lowered her head again, not looking at him but listening as he introduced the woman at his side. Her name was Amanda Delvaux, her accent unmistakably French, her smile charming yet faintly hostile.

Laura watched Amanda Delvaux curve her perfectly manicured hand over Tom Farrell's arm, her long tanned fingers stroking the expensive cloth of his jacket. It was a warning, possessive gesture to the two women at the table, subtly telling them that Tom Farrell belonged to her. It was difficult for Laura to ignore the conflict of emotion that raged inside her at such a thought. Was Amanda Delvaux his mistress? It seemed very likely.

Lost in thought, she did not participate in the conversation. She did not know what to say anyway. Tom Farrell was totally different from any man she had met before, she knew that instinctively, and there was a basic shyness in her nature that held her silent and observant as the others chatted. She looked at Amanda Delvaux and wondered what qualities in a woman held a man like Tom Farrell. She guessed that Amanda Delvaux was in her early thirities. She was beautiful, mature and very intelligent. Everything I'm not, Laura decided flatly, not knowing why it should matter. Tom Farrell, she guessed, was in his mid-thirties, maybe a little older. He would never *ever* be interested in a gauche twenty-three-year-old like herself.

Then they were leaving, and Laura felt Tom Farrell's eyes on her again. She forced herself to look at him, to smile into the heavy smoky depths of his eyes as she murmured her farewell.

He did not smile back, but stared at her, and she sensed a powerful stillness in him, and something else that she could not recognise, something abrupt and somehow violent. She pulled her eyes away, aware that her heart was pounding hurriedly, and smiled at Amanda Delvaux, who, surprisingly, smiled back, presumably relieved to be leaving. They walked away, a tall striking couple who turned heads as they moved through the crowded restaurant. Laura did not watch them go. She did not want Tom Farrell to leave and she certainly did not want to see him leaving with Amanda Delvaux.

Grace was watching them, though, easier for her because she was facing the door and Laura watched Grace, dying to know how she knew Tom Farrell. She could not remember Grace ever mentioning him before, although of course there was no reason why she should.

Grace's life had been troubled over the past eighteen months, with the soul-destroying deterioration of her marriage, and men, any man, did not figure strongly in her conversation. She was sick of them, she often told Laura, they were all the same. Laura could not really agree with this, but she could see the situation from Grace's point of view, only hoping that such bitterness would not mar her friend's life for too long.

Grace was smiling, her eyes reminiscent. 'Tom Farrell, fancy seeing him again—he doesn't change. And wasn't she lovely?'

'Who is he?' Laura asked, unable to contain her curiosity any longer.

'Tom Farrell, the playwright—surely you know the name.'

Laura did, of course. He was very well known, but she had been too shaken by the man himself to even think very much about his name. 'How do you know him?' she pressed.

Grace raised her eyebrows teasingly. 'I'm not sure I like the implications behind that question!'

'You know what I mean! The emphasis is on "how", not "you"!'

Both girls laughed and Grace explained, 'He was my tutor at drama school for six months—he was an actor then, of course. He helped me a lot, I remember he was an excellent tutor. Then about two years later, I did a play with him—we're not particular friends, but we bump into each other from time to time. Acquaintances is the word.'

Laura digested this information carefully, his image still crystal clear in her mind. She had forgotten that Grace had been an actress before she had had her children.

'Do you know Miss Delvaux?'

Grace shook her head. 'No—she's beautiful, though. Tom's never short of beautiful company. Even before he was famous, women used to be falling over each other to get to him. I wasn't immune myself,' she confided.

'Affair?' Even as she asked, Laura prayed that the answer would be no. Fortunately it was.

'I never got past the first post. He wasn't interested.'

Grace's eyes sharpened. 'Why all the questions?' Laura could not control the faint rush of colour to her cheeks. 'Ah, I see. I don't blame you, he is magnificent.'

'So is Amanda Delvaux,' Laura said flatly. 'What else do you know about him? Where is he back from?' Her questions tumbled unbidden from her mouth.

'And to hell with Amanda Delvaux,' Grace said softly. 'I heard that he was in France—his wife was involved in a skiing accident, I believe. . . .' Laura had already stopped listening, her brain blocking out Grace's voice. His wife. The words sang in her mind, a slow sad chant. How could it affect her so? She did not know him, he was a stranger, and besides, what had she expected? That a man like Tom Farrell would be free? Despite all her stern reasoning, all her self-admonishing, depression crept over her in a crazy illogical grey cloud.

'His wife?' She was barely aware of uttering the words, but Grace picked up on them immediately.

'Yes, he's married, but from what I hear, and there's plenty of gossip about it, as you can imagine, it's well and truly over, has been for years.'

'Why aren't they divorced, then?' Laura asked dully.

'Now that I don't know. Laura, is something wrong?'

Grace was concerned now and Laura shook her head quickly and automatically. Grace must be thinking that she was out of her mind, and even she was astounded by her own behaviour. An attractive stranger that she had glimpsed in a restaurant, been very briefly introduced to, turned out to be married. So what? It should not matter at all. But it did, and her mind raced over what Grace had said. She believed his marriage was over, yet he was not divorced and had just got back from visiting his wife in France. And besides all that, there was Amanda Delvaux, who had easily and successfully managed to give the impression of casual intimacy with him. She sighed heavily, knowing that she had to put Tom Farrell out of her mind and the sooner the better. She smiled at Grace and noticed a waiter staring at them rather fixedly. 'I think it's time to go if we're not ordering any food,' she whispered.

Grace turned her head and looked at the waiter. 'I think you're right.'

They paid for their drinks and collapsed giggling on the street as soon as they got outside. 'I thought we'd at least be shot at dawn,' Grace gasped. 'Did you see his face?'

'I could hardly fail to,' Laura replied, unable to control her giggling, wondering at the quality of hysteria in both their laughter.

'Well, that's another restaurant we can add to our list of places we daren't go to again,' Grace said shakily.

'Who cares? If there's one thing London is not short of, it's restaurants,' Laura replied airily.

'That won't last long at the rate we're going through them. Give us a year and I can see us having to drive down to Surrey for a hamburger!' Grace muttered, making them both laugh again.

Finally they sobered as they strolled along the busy street. The sun was bright and warm, the streets dusty, busy with people and traffic. Laura looked up at the blue sky. She could only see a tiny portion of it, the rest was blocked out by tall, dirty buildings. Suddenly she wanted to get out of the city, to go somewhere where she could see the horizon, somewhere flat and deserted.

'What are you going to do this afternoon?' she asked,

glancing into the shop windows they passed.

'I'd like to go home and see the kids,' Grace replied. 'I have a lot of thinking to do.'

'Of course.' Laura was concerned at the sadness in Grace's face.

'I'm in no mood to work today, would you mind if we put if off until tomorrow?' Grace was anxious not to offend.

'It suits me fine,' Laura reassured her. 'It's much too nice a day to work anyway. I'll ring you tomorrow morning to sort something out.'

They had reached Grace's tiny yellow car. 'I'm sorry, Laura, I didn't mean to be such a bore. Can I give you a lift back?'

'No, I'd rather like to walk—and don't be silly, you haven't been the least bit boring.' Laura touched her friend's arm lightly. 'I'll see you tomorrow.'

When Grace was gone, Laura stared into a shop window with unseeing eyes, worrying about her. Grace's meeting with the solicitors had obviously shaken her, but Laura did not know what to do to help. Grace needed to be alone to sort things out. She frowned. Grace and Nick had been so happy together when Laura had first met them. Jan had just been born and they had seemed to Laura the perfect family. Now their marriage was in ruins, Nick was living with his secretary and Grace was living alone, both waiting for the divorce that would free them from each other. It was depressing and miserable and did not fit in with Laura's romantic ideas of love.

She found herself wandering without thinking down the smaller back streets until she came to a small antique shop that she passed nearly every day. She looked into the window anxiously. It had not been sold, it still sat in the middle of the window display on a velvet-covered stand, sunlight shining off its silver surfaces, the enamels and precious stones glowing, almost unearthly bright. She came almost every day to this antique shop, to look at this Art Nouveau jewel casket, wishing and wishing that it was hers, but knowing that it would be a long time before she could afford it, and it was so perfect, so beautiful that it was bound to be sold before that time. She was not particularly materialistic, having only a very few possessions that meant a lot to her, and she was not naturally acquisitive, but something about this casket appealed to her deeply. Her eyes had been drawn to it almost by magic, the first day it had appeared in the window. She had stared at it for almost half an hour, noticing with delight the tiny engraved initials—L.D.—her own initials, on the clasp. She was attracted to it for some strange reason she could not explain and the initials seemed to be a message, some sort of prophecy, she thought fancifully. And she felt sure that the day she came past and it had been sold, the window suddenly empty, she would probably burst into tears on the street and make an utter fool of herself.

If only I had the money to buy it, she thought fiercely, so lost in her thoughts that she did not notice the tall man approaching her, nearly jumping out of her skin when a low, cool voice behind her said, 'Beautiful, isn't it?' His voice shivered along her spine like an icy finger and she spun round, wide-eyed, to find Tom Farrell staring down at her, smiling slightly. There was no sign of Amanda Delvaux, and she felt the betraying colour washing up over her face.

'I . . . I beg your pardon?' she faltered, shocked to see him.

'The silver casket,' he said softly, his narrowed grey eyes moving over her face.

'Oh, yes,' she said on a little sigh. 'It's lovely.' Then a thought struck her. 'Are you following me?'

He smiled again. 'Why should I be following you?'

His voice was curiously gentle and made her feel childish for asking such a ridiculous question. She turned away from him, her heart beating too fast and stared back into the shop window.

'Do you know anything about it?' she asked quietly, watching his reflection in the glass.

He moved beside her. 'Archibald Knox, 1901 or 1902, probably for Libertys,' he said, staring at her vulnerable profile.

She did not look at him, aware that he was watching her. For some reason she was not surprised by his knowledge. 'I think it must be the most beautiful box in the world,' she said rather sadly.

Tom Farrell laughed very softly. 'Do you want it?' he asked expressionlessly.

Her head jerked towards him, her eyes briefly meeting his and veering away, resting uncomfortably on the third button of his silk shirt. Was it as it seemed, or was he offering to buy it for her? If the latter, why?'

'I don't understand,' she murmured, held perfectly still by his nearness, his attraction.

'It's a perfectly straightforward question.' His voice coolly mocked her and she coloured, feeling inexplicably hurt.

'Yes, I want it,' she answered shortly. 'And if you'll excuse me, Mr Farrell. . . .' She wanted to get away. Suddenly she was out of her depth, and he was married, a fact that put him out of her reach permanently. But before she could move away he reached out a hand and caught her chin in firm yet gentle fingers, tilting up her pale face to his scrutiny.

Laura trembled at his touch, desperately tense. He

felt the tremor that ran through her and frowned.

'I've offended you,' he said gently, seriously. 'I'm sorry. I was clumsy, trying to rush things, I guess.' He smiled, his grey eyes becoming warm, charming and very persuasive. 'Will you have dinner with me tonight—a way of putting things right, making amends?'

Her heart leapt at his invitation, the force of his charm hard to resist until she remembered his wife. And as though that wasn't enough she also remembered Amanda Delvaux, and her spine stiffened.

'No, thank you, Mr Farrell,' she said stiltedly, wishing he would let her go, his long fingers seemed to be burning her skin.

'So shy and so formal,' he mused softly. 'Change your mind, Laura—who knows, you might even enjoy yourself.' He was teasing her, using her christian name for the first time and it sounded beautiful in his mouth.

She swallowed convulsively. She had to get away. This man had the power to destroy her, all her instincts had told her that the moment she had first seen him in the restaurant. He was worldly and experienced and she had no doubt that he was playing games with her, amusing himself at her expense. She lifted blank violet eyes to his hard face. 'I've said no, and I mean no, Mr Farrell. Now will you please let me go?' She tried to make her voice sound as cold as possible, but it shook alarmingly as she requested her release.

'As you wish.' He dropped his hand immediately, his dark brows drawing together frowningly. He seemed about to say something else, but Laura did not wait to hear, but turned on her heel and walked hurriedly away from him without saying goodbye. She glanced over her shoulder once or twice as she made her way home, but there was no sign of him, and her relief was mixed with a kind of haunting sadness that their meeting had been so disastrous, so embarrassing, and feeling that way made her angry with herself for being so vulnerable to his magnetic charm.

It would have been so easy to agree to have dinner with him and she had no doubt that he could easily have made her forget that he was married—he could have made her forget everything. She pushed a hand through her hair, realising for the first time that she was trembling. At least she would be home soon—the day seemed to have lasted for ever and it was only mid-afternoon.

Home was a large warehouse in Chelsea that had been converted into two huge flats, both with studios and workrooms. The ground floor flat was occupied by Gino Premoli, the owner of the building, a clever young artist who earned most of his money in advertising, and who was a good friend to Laura. She had first met him through her cousin Dee, who had at that time been renting the flat above Gino's. Laura had moved in with her cousin during her last term at college and by the time Dee had left to get married a year or so later, Laura found that with her newly increased income, she could afford to keep the flat on for herself. It cost a lot, more than she could really manage, but it was worth it because it was convenient for the city centre and it was big and spacious, and she enjoyed the freedom of living on her own.

She opened the black front door now and stepped inside with relief. Home at last! Gino was working in the huge hall, painting a mural on one of the walls. He smiled at her, then noticing her air of worried distraction, put down his brushes, wiped his hands and walked over to where she was idly flicking through her mail.

'You look worried, baby,' he said, flicking back a strand of her golden hair.

Laura wrinkled her nose at him. 'Very observant,' she answered with a smile. She liked Gino very much, he was bright and cheerful, and their relationship was uncomplicated and supportive. In his mid-twenties, he was tall and lean with black curly hair and a wide generous mouth. He had been born and brought up in England, sent to the best schools by wealthy Italian parents. She could hardly think of him as Italian, he seemed more English than she was, and she often teased him about that. He was brilliant at his job and very talented as an artist. More than that, he was a good person, a very good friend.

'So, invite me up for some coffee and tell me about it,' he suggested casually.

'Okay, come up.' They walked up the wide wooden staircase together. 'It's looking good,' Laura remarked, peering over the banister at his almost-finished mural.

'A masterpiece,' he replied darkly. 'And totally immovable.'

'You could always make a copy,' she said flippantly, knowing the blasphemy of such a suggestion. 'And there's always photos.'

Gino rolled his eyes in horror, making her laugh.

Once inside her flat she went straight to the kitchen to switch on the percolator. Gino watched her work.

'Tell me,' he prompted gently.

Laura smiled at him. 'I'm worried about Grace. I met her for lunch today and she was dreadfully upset. The divorce is going to be awful for her, I don't know how she'll cope. But what can I do to help? She can't even talk about it at the moment.'

'Just be there if she needs you—that's all you can

do,' said Gino, taking the tray from her and carrying it through into the enormous lounge-cum-studio. He placed it on a low tiled table and strolled over to her huge untidy desk. 'Can I look?'

'Help yourself.' Laura poured coffee for them both as he slowly and carefully examined her latest batch of illustrations.

For the past two years Laura had been working with Grace on children's books. Grace wrote and Laura illustrated—a perfect partnership that had been a fairly good commerical success. Laura was not rich by any means, but she could afford the flat and life's essentials and she could not imagine a nicer career.

'They're good,' Gino said finally. 'Strong and witty, I like them.'

'Thank you.' She greatly appreciated his praise, admiring his talent as she did, glad that he approved of her work. 'Come and sit with me and tell me what's been happening to you.'

They talked the rest of the afternoon away and Gino left at seven to change for a dinner date. Alone, Laura pulled down the brown blinds, switched on the television and made herself some cheese on toast. But for some reason she found that she could not concentrate on the screen in front of her. Tom Farrell's face rose strongly in her mind, all hard bones and shadowed hollows and mocking grey eyes. She tried to block him out, to think about something else, but he would not go. She moved restlessly around the room, thinking about him, remembering everything he had said to her, every movement of that lean powerful body. Then she told herself off loudly and very sternly, switched off the television and went to shower.

In her green-painted bathroom she quickly stripped off her clothes and stared at herself in the mirror, trying to see herself as Tom Farrell had seen her. The same person as usual stared back at her, tall and slim with a curved, graceful body, heavy blonde hair that curled around her shoulders and a small fine-boned face with deep violet eyes and a wide gentle mouth. Ordinary, she thought with dissatisfaction, totally unaware of her beauty. I'm certainly no competition for Amanda Delvaux.

That thought stopped her dead in her tracks. She should not want to compete with Amanda Delvaux. Tom Farrell was a married man and it was more than likely that she would never see him again. She showered hurriedly, then telephoned her mother and father in New York, where they had been living since her father retired. She was anxious to fill in her time, and it was good to speak to them again and to hear all their news.

Laura's elder sister had married an American businessman and lived there permanently. Wanting to be near their grandchildren and having nothing much to hold them in England after retirement, her parents had accepted Nancy's invitation to move over with her and her husband. At the time, Laura had considered going too, but had decided against it. She was still in college, working for her degree, and had felt at the time that she could not throw that up. And she liked England, so she had moved into this flat with Dee, which had satisfied her parents, who thought Dee 'a sensible girl', and stopped them worrying about her.

She visited her parents and her sister regularly but was now sure that she had made the right decision in staying in England. New York was fine in small doses, but the thought of living there all the time terrified her. Her mother told her that they would be flying over for Christmas, in between worried enquiries as to whether Laura was feeding herself properly. It was good news, but she still felt a bit lonely and cut off when she finally replaced the receiver.

Still restless and unsettled, she went to bed early. She did not sleep, but lay staring into the darkness wondering why on earth she could not put Tom Farrell out of her mind. What was happening to her?

CHAPTER TWO

LAURA got up late the next day after a dreadful, almost sleepless night. She felt hollow-eyed and depressed. She dressed uncaringly in jeans and a violet-coloured jumper, then sipped two cups of coffee, staring out of the windows at the dark and steady downpour of rain that suited her mood completely.

She did not want to move, but knew that she had to go round and see Grace about work on their latest book, so she telephoned Grace's house, dialling listlessly, and made arrangements to call. Grace sounded as miserable as Laura felt and she could hear the children screaming at each other in the background, so she agreed to call over right away. She was pulling on her jacket when Gino knocked on her door and entered, carrying a large parcel.

'This has just been delivered for you,' he announced cheerfully, placing it on one of the scarlet sofas.

'Thanks, Gino.' She could not muster up very much enthusiasm. She knew what the parcel contained anyway, fine drawing paper from the wholesaler, and in her present mood that was hardly a cause for riotous joy.

'Hey, Laura,' Gino came to stand in front of her, taking both of her hands in his, 'why so sad?' His eyes were kind and worried, and ridiculously she felt tears welling up in her eyes. 'I don't know,' she whispered, not quite truthfully. It had something to do with Tom Farrell, that she knew for sure, but exactly what, she had no idea. Gino sighed and put his arms round her, offering the comfort of a good friend. She relaxed against him and let her tears flow freely, glad that she was not alone. He held her until her tears stopped, then produced a slightly paint-smeared handkerchief and wiped her face before lightly kissing her mouth.

'Coffee?' he asked, with a slight smile.

Laura shook her head. 'I'm on my way out to Grace's. I promised to be there before noon.'

'I'll give you a lift.'

'Aren't you busy?'

'Not this morning,' he told her lightly.

It took them half an hour to reach Grace's house, the traffic was so busy, most of the journey being accomplished at a slow crawl. Laura was silent most of the way, listening to Gino as he talked, obviously trying to cheer her up.

Grace came to the door to meet them, and insisted that Gino come in for coffee. Laura was surprised at the untidiness of the house and shocked at Grace's appearance and obvious unhappiness.

The children were arguing in the sitting room, Jan in tears, wailing loudly and hitting her elder brother. She ran to Laura, hoping for sympathy from the new arrivals.

They chatted over coffee and then Gino offered to take the children to the park. Laura smiled at him gratefully, touched by his kindness, knowing that Grace needed a little peace. The children and Gino left in a storm of shouting and slamming doors and the silence that fell over the house on their departure seemed deafening.

Grace was chain-smoking, Laura noticed worriedly as she accepted a cigarette. She looked at her friend, noting Grace's bruised eyes and untidy brown hair, her nervous abrupt movements.

'Grace. . . .' she began tentatively, not wanting to say the wrong thing. 'Can't I help? Can't you talk about it?'

Grace's fingers played fast and nervously with the silver pendant at her throat, as she stared out of the window.

'I don't know what's happening to me,' she said in a low voice. 'I can't manage everyday things and I can't cope with the kids . . . my life seems to be in ruins.'

'Don't you want a divorce?' Laura probed gently, hoping that to talk would help.

'Yes, of course I do. I'm not still in love with Nick, if that's what you think. Oh, I don't know what it is! I feel as though I've failed everybody, not only Christy and Jan, but myself. What can I offer them as they grow up? Certainly not their father or a stable home life.'

'Oh, Grace!' Laura moved to sit by her side. 'They'll still be able to see Nick, and when they're old enough, they'll understand. Surely it's better for them to be brought up in a happy atmosphere with you alone, rather than with both of you, obviously unable to live together. All the arguments and tension and bitterness must damage children more than divorce. I'm not putting this very well, but you know what I'm saying, don't you?'

Grace turned from the window. 'Yes, and I appreciate all your help. I know my thinking isn't logical at the moment—it's just a black mood.' She sighed. 'I thought I loved Nick. I was sure I loved him, but what happened to that? Familiarity, boredom—you just drift along, not even noticing, and then one day you wake up and it's over, there's nothing left except knowledge of each other, fondness maybe. Would you believe, I didn't even care that Nick was having an affair with his secretary. Oh, I was angry at first, but when I examined that anger, I found that it was only hurt pride, not jealousy or pain. Crazy, isn't it?' She got to her feet jerkily and lit another cigarette. 'I need to get away from this house for a while. I feel it's closing in on me—it's too much to do with our marriage, too many memories I have no desire to remember.'

'Perhaps you should sell it,' Laura suggested, shaken by what Grace had told her. It was all so intense, so sad.

'I can't do anything until all the legalities are sorted out,' Grace said dully.

'You could come and stay with me, there's plenty of room.' The idea had only just occurred to her and she was anxious to help, her face bright with enthusiasm.

'Thanks for the offer, you don't know how I appreciate it, but I couldn't put you out like that, I really couldn't,' Grace said gently.

'It would be no trouble at all. I wouldn't have offered, would I?' Laura asserted. But Grace smiled.

'Well, if I'm honest, it's not only the house, it's London. Do you know what I'd really like to do? I'd like to go away to the country for a month or so, get away completely.'

'I wouldn't mind that myself. I've been thinking how dirty and claustrophobic the city is lately. I can't even see the sky properly,' Laura said sadly. 'Perhaps we could arrange something together, when Christy is on holiday, that is, if you didn't mind me coming with you.'

'It sounds like a great idea, but you mustn't come just because you feel worried or sorry for me,' Grace said firmly.

'I feel much too sorry for myself,' Laura replied

lightly, half-truthfully, Tom Farrell suddenly filling her thoughts. 'And I think it's high time we had a holiday.'

With that decided, both girls' moods were lighter. They had another cup of coffee, then started work. Grace approved of Laura's illustrations and they discussed the final chapter of their book together. By the time Gino brought the children back, it was well after lunchtime, and Laura prepared salad with cold meat and crusty bread for everybody. Over the meal, which was noisy and disorganised, Laura fondly watched Gino with Grace's children. They had loved him immediately, he had a special way with them. He caught her staring at him and raised his eyebrows, smiling, before his attention was diverted by Christy, who was trying to steal a slice of roast beef from Gino's plate but giving himself away because he was giggling so much.

As Laura washed up after lunch, Gino came to find her. 'I have to go, baby. I have a meeting with a client at three. Will you be able to find your own way back?'

'I'm not an idiot,' she replied pertly. 'Thanks for helping with the kids, Gino, and for the lift and everything.' She leaned forward and pressed her lips to his cheek, noticing as she drew back that his eyes had suddenly darkened and his smile had gone. He was staring at her, and she turned back to the sink in confusion. He touched her hair silently and left the room, and Laura finished the work with a frown creasing her forehead as she wondered at that look she had caught on his face. There had been an intensity in him that she had never seen before, and it made her nervous. Telling herself that she was probably imagining it all, she dried her hands and went to find Grace.

'Gino's forgotten his sweater.' Christy waylaid her

in the hall with this news, tugging at her arm. Before she had the chance to open her mouth, the doorbell rang. She took Christy's rather grubby hand.

'That will probably be Gino, remembering that he's left his sweater behind—let's go and see, shall we?'

'Can I open the door? Will you lift me up?'

Laura smiled at him. 'Of course you can, darling.' He was a strong, heavy child and it took nearly all her strength to lift him. The door swung open, both of them laughing. 'We thought. . . .' The words froze on her lips, her laughter dying as she stared into the enigmatic face of Tom Farrell.

'You're not Gino!' Christy accused loudly.

A faint smile softened the hard line of Tom Farrell's mouth. 'No, I'm not Gino,' he agreed quietly, as serious as the little boy.

Christy stared at him. 'Who are you, then?'

'I'm Tom, and you must be Christy.'

'Yes, I'm Christy,' the child answered importantly. Unable to hold him any longer, Laura lowered him to the ground, her arms aching, and he ran into the house chanting 'Tom! Tom! Tom!'

Laura suppressed a smile and lifted her violet eyes to Tom Farrell's face. He was watching her, his narrowed eyes sliding over her, taking in her tousled hair, her small face, free of make-up, and her tight jeans. She felt herself colouring under his slow scrutiny and lowered her eyes.

'Is Grace out?' he asked softly, faintly mocking, and Laura realised that she had made no move to let him into the house.

'I . . . I'm sorry, Mr Farrell . . . er . . . Grace is in the sitting room . . . come in. . . .' she stammered, stepping back to allow him entrance.

'Thank you.' His voice was openly amused as he

moved past her. 'How are you, Miss Drake?' His deliberate use of her surname seemed to mock her own stilted formality and her mouth tightened.

'Very well, thank you, *Mr* Farrell,' she replied in a stiff little voice, cursing her heart for beating so fast, cursing the dryness in her mouth.

'I'm glad.' He sounded perfectly serious.

'Please don't make fun of me,' she said rather desperately, realising as the words were uttered that she was being silly and childish.

Tom Farrell sighed, his eyes darkening on her flushed face. 'Laura,' he began gently.

'Tom! Christy told me you were here—come in.' Grace's voice broke between them as she stepped into the hall.

Tom Farrell turned his dark head and smiled at her. 'I've broought the books you asked for.'

Laura moved past him quickly. 'Shall I make some coffee?' she asked no one in particular, her voice stained and artifically bright.

Once in the kitchen she plugged in the percolator and sat down at the table, pressing a trembling hand to her forehead. What had possessed her to act so stupidly? Why couldn't she be polite but distant with him, then none of this embarrassment would arise?

She made yet another pot of coffee and composing her face into a calm mask, carried the tray into the sitting room. Tom Farrell was talking to Grace, but his eyes flicked over her as soon as she entered the room. She sat as far away from him as possible, trying to still the trembling of her hands as she poured out three cups of coffee.

'How do you take your coffee, Mr Farrell?' she asked politely, marvelling at how steady her voice sounded.

'Black, no sugar.' He smiled at her and her stomach

tightened fiercely. She handed Grace a cup, then strolled over to Tom Farrell. Their fingers touched very briefly as the china cup changed hands and Laura drew back as though scalded, knowing that he had not missed her reaction.

Then she was safely back in her seat, watching him covertly over the rim of her cup. He looked incredibly attractive in tight jeans and a blue checked shirt. Her pulses raced hotly just to look at him. He exuded an aura of leashed power, of complete self-assurance, charisma and magnificent virility. He was hard and confident and probably cruel, Laura decided, frightened of his power, his sharp intelligence, not liking him very much at that moment. He saw too much, especially when it came to her. He could strip away her very fragile defence, just by assessing her with his cool grey eyes. But worse than that was the way he attracted her, making her hungry to see him, to know him.

Panicking, she wanted to get away, so she got to her feet and smiled stiffly at Grace. 'I have to go, Grace. I've got some ideas for that chapter, so I'll do some drawings tonight and telephone you tomorrow.'

'I'll give you a lift back,' Grace said, her expression surprised, her eyes questioning.

The man at her side glanced at the gold watch on his wrist and moved gracefully to his feet. 'I have to be leaving myself, so I'll be happy to give Miss Drake a lift home,' he drawled softly.

Grace flashed him a brilliant smile. 'Thanks, Tom, it's very kind of you.'

'It's no trouble at all.' His eyes lingered disturbingly on Laura's mouth as he spoke.

She wanted to protest that she did not have to have a lift home arranged for her. She was more than capable of getting back under her own steam, but did not want to upset Grace, so she decided to wait until they got outside, then she would tell Tom Farrell what he could do with his lift. A slight smile touched the corners of her mouth. She wouldn't, of course, she would just turn down his offer politely but firmly.

Once outside Tom Farrell slipped his hand lightly beneath her elbow and guided her towards a long black car parked outside the gate. His touch, impersonal though it was, disturbed her, weakening her resistance to him. She stood by the car whilst he unlocked the passenger door, and licked her lips nervously.

'If . . . if you don't mind, I'd rather get the bus,' she said quickly, before her courage failed her.

'Why?' He turned towards her, folding his arms across his broad chest and staring down at her.

The question floored her. She could not answer it without sounding downright rude.

'I just think it would be better,' she muttered inanely.

'For whom? For you, waiting for God knows how long for a bus that won't take you anywhere near? Or for me?' he enquired coldly.

She saw the tension in him and was frightened by it. 'Why are you so angry?' she asked, in a small voice.

'Why the hell are you so childish?' he snapped abruptly. Then, 'Laura, I'm offering you a lift, nothing more, nothing less. Why are you making such a big issue of it?'

She frowned at him. 'I'm *not* making a big issue of it. I don't know you and I don't understand why you're offering me a lift, that's all.' She was aware of how obstinate she was being, but she could not help herself.

'Because you're a friend of Grace's and I happen to like Grace. Okay?' He opened the passenger door.

'Now get in and shut up.' His anger was gone as quickly as it had come, and he smiled at her as he gave the order. Laura's heart twisted as she did as he said, sliding gracefully into the low leather seat. Seconds later he slid in beside her, still smiling, and offered her a cigarette.

'You're such a stubborn child,' he murmured, as he lit the cigarette for her.

'I'm not a. . . .' She bit off her hasty retort and drew on the cigarette. It was useless to argue with him. He was a man who always got his own way, and she couldn't swim against the tide for ever. She gave him her address and settling down in her seat, smoked in silence as he manoeuvred the sleek car into the traffic.

He was silent, seemingly preoccupied as he drove, and Laura looked at his hands on the steering wheel. They were very strong, tanned and long-fingered, but despite the power in them she could imagine them being incredibly gentle. She closed her eyes, disturbed and strangely excited by her thoughts. She wondered what his plays were like. Perhaps she would ask Grace, or better still, she could borrow them from the local library. Her eyes slid surreptitiously to his profile. It was hard, uncompromising, a strong, well-defined jaw, shadowed hollows beneath his cheekbones, dark eyelashes, gleaming black hair. She looked away quickly, filled with an emotion she did not understand. The silence seemed to grow until she could hear her own breathing, her own heartbeat, both sounding unnaturally loud. Could he hear them too?

'Mr Farrell. . . .' she began tentatively.

'Tom,' he cut in firmly.

'I . . . er. . . .'

'Say it.'

She swallowed. 'Tom.' Her voice was low, husky, a warm caress.

'That's better. What were you going to say?' he asked gently.

'I don't know, I've forgotten,' she admitted, laughter in her voice. Amazingly, he laughed too, and the tension was eased. Five minutes later the car slid to a silent halt outside the warehouse. Tom Farrell turned slightly in his seat, watching her with smoky eyes.

'Th—thank you for the lift,' she whispered.

'Why are you afraid of me?' His voice was expressionless.

'I'm not,' she replied without conviction, unable to look at him.

'You are.' He leaned forward and gently touched the pulse that beat far too fast in her throat. 'And your heart gives you away, little one.'

She pushed his hand from her bare skin, where it burned like a brand, hating him for his cleverness. 'Don't touch me!' she flashed angrily, using her anger as her only defence against him. His mouth tightened and he reached for her, his fingers closing steel-strong on her shoulders, turning her to face him in the expensive, intimate confines of the car. He was not hurting her, but she was well aware that if she tried to move away his fingers would remorselessly bruise her delicate bones.

'Payment for the ride?' she queried, proud and scornful. She heard the hiss of his indrawn breath.

'Dear God, Laura, you try my patience,' he muttered harshly. 'Why are you fighting this?'

She knew what he was talking about, of course, he was talking about the fierce attraction between them, the electric tension, the sweet excitement that locked them together whenever they looked at each other. But she couldn't admit that to him. Not now, not ever.

'I don't know what you're talking about,' she said, almost steadily, her violet eyes still downcast.

'You're a liar.' He caught her chin between his fingers and forced her to look at him.

Her breath caught in her throat as she stared into his shadowed eyes. 'Let me go,' she muttered brokenly, her breath coming sharply as her gaze dropped to the hard warm line of his mouth. It was more than a request for him to take his hands from her, they both knew that.

'I can't.' His voice was low, vibrant.

Laura twisted futilely in his grasp, afraid of the whirlpool of feelings he was arousing in her. 'I hate you,' she muttered with passionate intensity.' 'And I wish you'd leave me alone!'

'Laura——' He stopped her with his mouth, parting her lips with a hunger that melted her resistance, like flame on ice, making her yielding and responsive, her slim arms creeping up around his neck, her fingers threading through the thick darkness of his hair. His mouth moved endlessly against hers, his kiss deepening, as anger left him, hardening with a desire that was as sudden as it was uncontrollable.

Laura had never been kissed with such intensity, such demand, before, and she responded completely, her lips moving innocently beneath the warmth of his. His hands left her shoulders to frame her face as his mouth left hers, moving across her fragile cheekbones, her forehead, closing her eyes with warm, gentle kisses, finally teasing the corner of her mouth with his tongue before slowly raising his head and looking down at her.

For a long moment Laura just stared back at him, dazed and aroused by the raw desire she saw in his brilliant eyes. He was breathing deeply, as she was, still holding her face tenderly between his hands.

'I can't leave you alone, you see,' he murmured with a slight smile. 'You've been on my mind ever since we met yesterday. I want you, Laura, and I don't think you can fight it any more than I can.'

She stiffened, jerking free of his hands, fighting the weak sensual lethargy in her stomach and suddenly coming to her senses. Was this the usual line he used? she wondered painfully. He was a married man, even if he didn't act like one, and she had no intention of getting involved with him.

'Oh, I can fight it, just watch me. You're married,' she said flatly, furiously. 'And I don't want an affair with you. You must think I'm really stupid! Well, you'd better wake up to the fact that I'm not going to fall for your clever lines, Mr Farrell, and I don't want to see you again. Do you understand?' Her voice was becoming perilously high as her words poured out and before she broke down, and not waiting to hear any answer from him, she fumbled with the handle on the door and pushing it open, jumped from the car and walked to the front door, without looking back.

She was just fitting her key into the lock when she heard the roar of the car engine and the protesting squeal of tyres as the car shot away. Bemused and very shaken, she walked up the stairs to her flat. The building was silent, empty—Gino was still out, she supposed, and she suddenly felt lonely again, miserable and worried. Grace, Tom Farrell, problems, problems....

She flung her bag and jacket on the sofa and made some tea, then, unable to sit still, lit a cigarette and stood by the window staring at the sky as she sipped her tea. Although she fought against it, she found herself thinking of Tom Farrell and the hungry touch of his mouth on her own. He had not lied, even though she had told him differently. She was attracted to him, no man had ever affected her so deeply, she had known that in the restaurant. But he was married, and nothing would persuade her to become involved with him, however much she ached to. It was wrong, and nothing could change that. She moved restlessly, wishing she had someone to talk to about Tom Farrell. But even if there had been somebody, would she have been able to talk freely about something so personal? Shy by nature, she doubted it.

She paced the floor miserably. She did not even have a steady boy-friend at present. She went out casually with men she knew, but although one or two had expressed a desire for a deeper, closer relationship, Laura had backed away. She felt nothing more than fondness for any of them, and the disastrous relationships of friends warned her away from any special commitment without love.

The telephone began to ring, intruding into her maudlin thoughts, and she was glad of the interruption. It was Joss Beckett, her agent, asking her out to dinner that night—he wanted to talk, he said, and Laura, desperately in the mood for company, readily agreed, spending the rest of the rapidly-fading afternoon in the bath, soaking luxuriously, deliberately keeping her mind blank to everything except the pleasure of the scented water.

When she was finally forced out of the bath, she spent an hour drying her hair and plaiting it carefully into an elaborate style that made the most of the fragile bone structure of her face and the graceful sweep of her neck. Then she made up her face and chose a slinky black dress with a matching jacket as her outfit for the dinner-date.

The intercom buzzed at exactly seven-thirty—Joss was always on time—and, ready for at least ten minutes, Laura grabbed her handbag, switched off the lights and slamming shut the door, ran downstairs, smiling as she tugged open the heavy front door.

'Ready, my dear?' Joss's blue eyes were alight with pleasure as he bent forward and kissed her cheek. 'You look delightful.'

'Thank you.' Laura took his arm as they strolled to where his car was parked. 'You look very smart yourself.' He was wearing a cream linen suit with a darker shirt and tie. He looked dignified and perhaps a little eccentric, his shaggy mane of silver hair neatly brushed, a dark red flower in the lapel of his jacket, certainly very much younger than his sixty years.

Joss laughed, flattered, and opened the passenger door of his ancient but perfectly-maintained Bentley, and Laura slid inside, glad to be going out for the evening. The restaurant was a favourite of Joss's, quiet and expensive, and they were sipping pre-dinner drinks at their table, waiting for their meal, chatting together, when he suddenly said, 'I bumped into Tom Farrell this morning.'

Laura's head jerked upwards. 'Tom Farrell?' she could not hide her surprise.

'You met yesterday, I believe,' Joss said, far too blandly for Laura's liking.

Her mind immediately began working overtime, suspicions forming easily.

'Yes, I met him yesterday,' she conceded flatly. 'I had no idea you knew him.'

Joss laughed. 'Known him for years, my dear. Everybody knows Tom Farrell.'

'Oh.' Laura's face closed and she sipped her drink a little too quickly. Was there no escape from that man?

she wondered almost desperately. Since the moment she had first seen him, her every waking moment seemed to have been dominated by him. It was all vaguely depressing.

'Sore point?' Joss asked shrewdly.

'Why should it be?' She was sure that the sudden colour in her cheeks was giving her away.

'You tell me,' he suggested wickedly.

Laura quickly changed the subject, but the thought that Joss and Tom Farrell had known each other for years nagged away at her intriguingly, as they ate the delicious food that the restaurant was renowned for. In the end curiosity got the better of her.

'Why did you mention Tom Farrell?' she asked, trying to keep her voice casual.

Joss flashed her a searching glance which for some reason irritated her. She had the feeling he was holding something back. 'No reason particularly—the fact that he's now a mutual acquaintance, I suppose.'

'I don't like him,' Laura said very firmly, stabbing her fork into the slice of cheescake in front of her, her appetite suddenly gone.

Joss raised his silver eyebrows. 'Such vehemence! It's not like you to take such a positive dislike to somebody you hardly know,' he said mildly, giving her an open invitation to talk, to confide, which Laura took.

She had known Joss ever since she had been at college. He was a very good friend, as well as her agent, almost like a second father, in fact.

'I know, I can't think what it is, probably the fact that I find him so damned attractive,' she said, attempting to joke but failing miserably.

'And what's wrong with that?' Joss asked amusedly.

'The fact that he's married, for a start,' Laura said flatly.

'The relationship he has with Julia is hardly what one would call a marriage. It's common knowledge, surely you've heard about it.'

'Grace did say something,' Laura mumbled, suddenly feeling that the whole conversation was rather cheap and sordid. Whatever the gossip, only Tom Farrell and his wife knew the true situation and no amount of talk could change the basic facts. She smiled at Joss. 'Let's not gossip. Tell me what you wanted to talk about.'

So yet again the conversation was steered away from Tom Farrell and Laura was left with an unsatisfied ache inside herself. It was almost as though she was afraid to know too much about him. Did she want to think of him as a philanderer in order to kill off the feelings she unwillingly found she had for him? Facts were facts, she told herself firmly, and concentrated on what Joss was talking about—an offer of work, twenty illustrations and a cover, for a book of children's poetry. She was interested but could not focus her entire concentration on his proposition, her thoughts veering off on vague tangents. Angry with herself, she agreed to do the work without thinking it out properly, glad to be able to please Joss, who seemed keen for her to accept, and hoping that the project would involve her completely for at least two months—plenty of time to rout Tom Farrell from her mind, she prayed.

She told Joss about her plan to spend a month or so in the country with Grace.
'It will do you good,' he told her. 'You're far too pale.'

All in all it was a pleasant evening and she arrived home feeling a good deal happier. She invited Joss in for coffee and they talked about her work while he looked over her illustrations for Grace's book. He told her that he was looking for a new housekeeper and made her laugh with witty anecdotes about the unsuitable applicants he had already interviewed.

He lived alone in a huge old house near Regent's Park, having never married. Laura knew little about his life, he was a very private person who could not talk easily about himself. She often wondered why he had never married, since he adored the company of women. He was an enigma, but a very nice one, and she valued his friendship highly.

The next day, quite by chance, she found one of Tom Farrell's plays on Gino's bookshelves, while she was looking through for a book he had promised to lend her. Tom's name leapt out at her and she took down the play with slightly trembling hands. She asked Gino if she could borrow it and took it upstairs, pushing aside her work to start reading it immediately. It took her all afternoon to read it and she found herself totally absorbed, not even hearing the telephone when it rang.

He was a brilliant, startling writer, witty, disturbing, shrewdly ambiguous and very, very clever. Things that she had only glimpsed in his cool grey eyes became clear—the depth of his character, the force of his personality. He was a strong special person with an insight, a piercing clarity of vision and an understanding of people that frightened her a little, it was so powerful.

As she turned the last page, read the final line, she felt close to tears, strangely drained yet at the same time happy, completed. He was a master of catharsis, she thought, as she scrubbed absently at her tears with the back of her hand and noticed that the room was in darkness except for the work-light over her desk that she had been reading by.

It was evening, the day had slipped by while she had lost herself completely in his play. She made some supper and spent the rest of the time before she went to bed curled up in a chair, unable to get the play or the man out of her mind. If she had hoped to lose her interest in him, reading one of his plays had been the worst mistake she could have made. She was even more intrigued by him, drawn to him now, God help her.

CHAPTER THREE

Two days later, Laura noticed that the silver casket had disappeared from the antique shop window. She was walking past, her mind on other things, deep in thought, when her eye registered the fact that the box had gone. She stopped dead in her tracks, her attention suddenly focusing on the plate glass, and her heart sank right down to her toes and ridiculously, as she had imagined days before, her eyes filled with tears.

She tried to picture the casket in a room, in a house somewhere, but couldn't. Stupid to get so worked up over a lump of metal, but she couldn't help herself. It belonged to *me*, she kept thinking, as she walked home, dragging her feet and feeling depressed.

As she stepped into the large hall and pushed shut the front door, she knew that there was something different about the place. Then she noticed that the huge mural was finished, giving the hallway a completed look, at exactly the same moment as Gino appeared, clutching a bottle of wine, his face wreathed in smiles.

'What do you think of it?' he demanded excitedly, walking over to her and slipping his arm around her shoulder, hugging her against him in his exuberance.

Laura laughed, infected by his mood, and slid her own arm around his waist. 'Strange and beautiful—I love it,' she said, after a moment's consideration. It seemed to alter the dimensions of the gigantic room, the startling colours reflecting on the ceiling, the pale walls, flickering with their own life, like an enormous fire.

'Really?'

'Yes, really,' she smiled, very impressed.

Gino held up the bottle of wine. 'A celebration seems in order,' he said. 'Your place or mine, or shall we have it right here?'

'Let's have it here, so that we can look at the mural while we celebrate,' Laura said gravely, then burst out laughing. Gino's happiness had completely banished her depression and she felt like doing something a little mad to lighten her serious mood. So Gino brought two chairs, two glasses and a radio from his flat into the hallway and pulled open the front door to let in sunlight and air, the smell of paint being still rather strong. Then while he opened the wine, Laura fiddled with the radio until she found a jazz piano which she turned up loud. Gino handed her a glass of red wine.

'A toast,' she said, managing to keep her face straight. 'To you, Gino,' and their glasses touched and Gino bowed slightly, his dark eyes flashing with amusement.

'To both of us, and the work of art before us,' he amended.

They drank their wine ceremoniously. Laura's foot was tapping in time to the music and Gino took her glass and placed it with his own on the floor.

'Dance?' he enquired, perfectly seriously.

'My pleasure,' Laura replied, extravagantly, moving into his arms. It was a crazy, improvised dance, made up as they went along, both laughing uncontrollably, caught up in the moment of madness, neither noticing the tall figure of a man in the doorway, moving silently into the hall and leaning indolently against the wall, watching the dancing couple, until Laura turned her head and stiffened in Gino's arms, as her eyes met the cold mocking gaze of Tom Farrell.

Gino turned then too, his hands still at Laura's waist. 'Hi, can I help you?' he shouted over the music.

'It's Laura I'm here to see,' Tom Farrell replied expressionlessly, not raising his voice at all.

Gino released her immediately and moved to turn down the radio. It was as though something in Tom Farrell's voice had warned him away from her, Laura thought irrationally, flushing under that slow, blank, grey gaze. Both men were waiting for her to make some positive move, tension buzzing round them, so she smoothed down her slinky knitted top and pushed back her golden hair with nervous hands.

'Would you like to come up?' She indicated the stairs to her flat. It was perfectly clear that Tom had no intention of talking in front of Gino, he had already somehow dismissed the younger man, she thought irritably.

She flashed Gino a warm, apologetic smile. 'Sorry, will you excuse me?'

He shrugged, his eyes serious. 'Sure.' Then he smiled back at her, showing her that he was not offended.

Tom Farrell was silent, close behind her as she led the way. As soon as they entered the lounge she walked quickly over to the windows, anxious to put some distance between them, then she turned and forced herself to look at him, her heart beating very fast.

'Did you have to be so rude to Gino?' she demanded, still angry.

'Was I rude?' he parried smoothly, mockingly, his piercing eyes telling her not to be so foolish.

Laura sighed. She could not fight him. Her eyes slid over him unknowingly. He looked dark and dangerous, overpoweringly attractive in tight faded jeans and a dark sweater, and he was staring at her, that same blankness in his face, almost as though he was asleep, she thought nastily. Unfortunately she knew the power of the mind behind that closed face, and it frightened her. He filled the room, it seemed, with his masculine presence as he stood so still and silent, reminding her of some powerful predator, hypnotising its victim before the kill.

She shivered, despite the heat in her skin and perversely wished that she was wearing something a little more elegant than the tight jeans that left the long smooth curve of hip and thigh open to his inspection.

'Why . . . why have you come here?' she demanded, her voice high and sharp in her tension, her nervous desire to break the silence.

'To talk,' he replied in that same smooth, expressionless voice.

'I don't think we have anything to say to each other,' she mumbled, lowering her head, hiding behind the silky curtain of her hair.

'You know that's not true.'

Laura swallowed nervously. 'Would you like some tea?' It was not that she wanted him to stay, but it would give her a chance to escape to the kitchen for a few moments, badly-needed time to pull herself together.

'Yes, thank you.' He smiled slightly and Laura almost bolted from the room.

She took her time in the kitchen, but the tea was ready faster than ever before, and in the end she was forced back into the lounge, her hands trembling so much that the china cups on the tray were actually rattling.

Tom Farrell was standing by her untidy desk, glancing through the pile of finished paintings for

Grace's book. He turned slowly as she entered the room then moved silently to take the tea tray from her.

Laura stared at him, her mouth dry, watching the strong lines of his face, the sunlight gleaming on his dark hair. She remembered with painful clarity the touch of that hair beneath her fingers, thick, vital, very erotic. She looked away quickly and sat down as far away as she possibly could.

Tom poured tea for them both. 'Do you take milk, sugar?' he asked quietly.

'Just milk, please,' she answered in a small voice.

He strolled over and handed her the cup, then moved away, sitting down opposite to her. A strange, tense ritual, and in the silence they could hear Gino whistling outside.

'Boy-friend?' Tom queried, his firm mouth twisting slightly.

'Is it any of your business?' Laura parried, determined to be difficult.

'I'm making it my business,' he smiled, taking the arrogance out of the words.

'Gino's a friend, a good friend, and that's all. He lives downstairs,' she heard herself answering truthfully.

The grey eyes held hers, openly cynical. 'I doubt if he's happy with that.'

Laura frowned. 'What does that mean?'

'You really don't know, do you?' He managed to sound totally unconvinced.

'I certainly don't know what you're talking about,' she snapped, sensing criticism, and took a mouthful of tea, finding it boiling hot and nearly choking.

'He's in love with you,' Tom told her flatly. Laura's eyes widened, pure deep violet, very shocked, as the implications of his words sank in.

Tom Farrell stared at her, his attention completely captured by her beauty. She shook her head dazedly. 'No ... no, I don't believe it. .. you're wrong ... you must be. ...' she faltered.

'Don't be ridiculous, little one, you know damned well that I'm right.' There was a strange anger in his voice and in his eyes, and she realised that in a way she did know. She might not have consciously admitted it to herself, but she knew. She remembered the way Gino had looked at her in Grace's kitchen. She had caught him off guard, and although it had gone in a second, it had lingered disturbingly in her mind for hours. She didn't want Gino to love her, and she certainly didn't want to hurt him.

'What shall I do?' she whispered, appealing for Tom Farrell's help.

'Don't be too kind to him,' he replied quite gently. It was not the answer she had hoped for.

'How do you know I'm not in love with him?' she asked angrily, wondering how he dared to burst into her life and tell her things she did not want to know. The cruel arrogance of the man! He had ruined for ever the simple beauty of her friendship with Gino, it would never be the same again. She would have to be cautious, careful not to encourage him wrongly; it was broken, ruined and terribly sad.

'I saw you dancing together downstairs just now—I know you're not in love with him,' Tom replied with calm, utter certainty.

Laura regretted the impulsive question. It had been foolish and he could make her feel foolish so easily. He needed no help from her. 'Do you have a cigarette?' she asked distractedly, running her hand through the thick silk of her hair, her mind still wrestling with the bombshell he had dropped.

Silently he lit two and handed her one, which she drew on deeply. 'Why did you tell me?' she demanded wearily. 'What possible good can it do?' She stared at him with wide, sad eyes, hating him at that moment because he seemed so destructive, so uncaring.

He sighed heavily. 'For your sake, but more for his, it's better that you know. I think you already knew deep down. I didn't mean to hurt you, Laura.'

She gazed into the shadowed depths of his eyes and suddenly trusted him, knew with a fierce twisting of her heart that she would even have trusted him with her life. It was an astounding self-revelation and one that immediately put her on the defensive.

'Why are you always right?' she asked irritably.

He laughed at that, a low pleasant growl of amusement. 'You wouldn't believe it,' he drawled softly, meaningfully.

She smiled. 'I'm sure I would.' Stubbing out her cigarette she said, 'What have you come to talk about?' Enough had been said about Gino, she would have to sort it out in her own mind when she was alone. She knew her thoughts about Tom Farrell had been unjust. Of course he had not ruined her friendship with Gino, he had probably saved Gino a lot of pain, by verifying Laura's suspicions. He had been right, however loath she was to admit it.

'Business,' he said crisply, his eyes narrowing on her face as his mood changed.

'What sort of business?' All her old suspicions flooded back. What was he up to?

'I've been looking at your work and I like it. I'm offering you a commission,' he said in a hard impersonal voice. He was being brief and to the point, his face totally blank.

Laura's first instinct was to refuse. Her heart told

her that if she deliberately involved herself with this man she would be courting disaster. He attracted her so much that she would be badly hurt. On the other hand, her head, her businesslike brain and the artist in her, were all intrigued, interested in the prospect of a new project, flattered that a man of Tom Farrell's brilliance should want her to work for him.

She could not hide the conflict inside her; warring emotions flitted through her dark eyes like a cinematic film. Tom watched her carefully, almost able to read her thoughts, her small face was so expressive, but he remained silent, even though he could so easily have influenced her with a couple of well-chosen words, persuaded her to do anything he asked.

'What sort of commission?' she finally asked, with extreme caution.

A slight smile pulled at the corners of his mouth. She was staring at him like a very sweet, very wary child. 'One illustration, a frontispiece for a play that's being published,' he explained briefly.

'One of your plays?' she asked in amazement.

'Of course. Are you accepting, little one?' His voice was gentle.

Laura thought about the play she had read and felt a fierce stab of excitement at the thought of being involved, however distantly, with his work. She knew in her heart that she had already decided, the moment he had asked. Her feelings were already too deep for her to fight them. She wanted any contact she could get with him. And besides all that, it was a wonderful career opportunity.

She took a deep breath. 'Yes, I accept. I'll be honoured to do the illustration for you,' she said gravely.

He moved towards her, swift and silent and bent over,

tracing the delicate line of her chin with gentle fingers. 'You're very sweet, very serious, and so lovely that you tear at my heart,' he murmured softly, almost to himself, as he traced the line of her mouth with his thumb.

She quivered, deeply affected by his words, her skin turning to fire where he touched it. She wanted his kiss more than anything in the world at that moment, wanted to turn her lips into the palm of his hand. She closed her her eyes, frightened at the warm ache of desire in her stomach, moving her head slightly so that his hand dropped.

'When . . . when shall I start?' she asked shakily.

'As soon as possible. Are you working on anything at the moment?' The grey eyes were shuttered again, blank and businesslike, his voice brisk.

'No.' She shyly indicated the pile of illustrations on her desk. 'I've just finished Grace's book, so I'm as free as a bird and can start whenever suits you.'

Tom smiled at her enthusiasm. 'You're very talented—I was looking at them before, I hope you don't mind, and I'm very glad you accepted the work.'

'Thank you.' Stunned by his praise, Laura was lost for words. The whole meeting, his proposition, everything, seemed totally unreal, she was floating on a cloud of dreams.

Tom threw back his tea in one mouthful. 'I'll give you a copy of the play and the rest is up to you.'

'There's nothing you particularly want?' She was very anxious to please, to do the right thing.

'You're the artist, it's entirely up to you,' he repeated quietly.

'I don't. . . .' she began, but he cut across her, reading her mind. 'There's no chance that you'll make a mistake, I've enough faith in you to know that.' That calm certainty threaded his voice again and Laura believed him, her confidence blossoming. Her mind was suddenly racing, alive with possibilities.

Tom watched her for a moment, then said, 'We should discuss payment, a contract.'

Laura shrugged absently, not really interested in money. 'Joss usually handles that sort of thing for me.'

'Joss Beckett?'

'Yes, you know him, I believe.' She was still vague, miles away.

Tom nodded. 'I'll ring him this afternoon.' He paused and lit another cigarette with smooth easy movements, offering her one which she refused, then he continued, 'I have something that I'd like to give you—to seal the agreement. Will you accept it?'

'What is it?' She was intrigued.

'I don't have it with me, so you'll have to wait and see.' He smiled, getting to his feet with that slow, indolent grace that riveted her eyes. 'Will you have lunch with me tomorrow? I'll have talked with Joss and the publishers by then, so we'll be able to talk over the final details. I'll also bring a copy of the play— and your bribe,' he added wickedly.

He was suggesting a business lunch, and as much as Laura wanted to agree, part of her held back. 'I don't know. . . .' she prevaricated, still slightly suspicious.

'Please, Laura.' His eyes were warm, his voice low and persuasive. 'Purely business, I assure you.'

'Okay.' She tried to sound casual and failed, her dark eyes giving her away.

'I'll pick you up at twelve-thirty.'

'Yes, fine.' She walked past him to open the door, but his hand closed on her shoulder, turning her to face him.

She looked up into his strong face, into his cool grey

eyes, and her breath caught in her throat, powerful, unrecognised emotion clutching at her heart. Tom slowly lowered his dark head, his warm mouth touching hers in a brief gentle caress. Then he was gone, leaving her shaken and bemused and absurdly happy. She stood staring after him for a moment, then shut the door and almost danced round the room. Carrying the tea tray into the kitchen, she washed up, singing loudly. She was *dying* to tell somebody her good news—she would tell Gino.

She rushed downstairs to his flat. The door was open, but she knocked anyway. 'Come in,' he shouted from within, and she followed his voice, finding him crosslegged on the floor in front of the windows, cleaning brushes. The room was crammed with enormous canvases, vivid with colour, the smell of paint strong and pleasant to her. The furniture too was bright, unusual, mostly designed and made by friends, fellow artists. It was a fascinating room, always full of light and life.

Gino looked up from his work and smiled at her. 'He's gone?' There was a faint harshness in his voice.

'Yes. I'm sorry, Gino, I was dreadfully rude, I didn't even introduce you. It's just that ... that....' She shrugged, unable to find the right words. 'He always disconcerts me, puts me off guard somehow.'

'I see,' Gino said drily, wiping his hands and jumping to his feet.

'No, you don't,' she said sadly. She thought of what Tom Farrell had said about Gino and felt like crying. She stared into the darkness of his eyes and saw nothing but kindness and friendship and warmth. When they were together like this she would have sworn that he did not love her. So why was she so certain that he did?

'Who is he anyway?' Gino turned away as he asked, collecting the huge pile of clean brushes, his voice a little too light, a little too casual.

'Tom Farrell,' she said blankly.

'Of course! I thought I recognised him, couldn't put a name to the face, though. You *are* going up in the world,' he teased, while his eyes questioned in silence.

'He's offered me some work,' Laura explained, answering the unspoken question, wanting to share her good luck with him. 'A frontispiece for one of his plays.'

'That's great, congratulations!' She did not miss the relief in Gino's eyes as he moved to hug her tightly. She hugged him back, miserable that now she knew how he felt, she was noticing things, tiny irrelevant things, that would never have occurred to her before. Damn Tom Farrell, she thought irrationally, even though she knew that it was not his fault, that he had done the right thing in opening her eyes. She clung tightly to Gino, glad of the lean reassurting hardness of his body, until he put her away from him, gently but firmly.

'What is it?' he questioned quietly, but she shook her head and averted her eyes. She could not tell him. 'Let's go out tonight, baby, a double celebration—your commission and my mural. It'll cheer you up.'

She thought for a moment, still unbearably confused, wondering if it was wise, then said, 'Yes, I'd like that.' It was a day for flying close to the sun, for reckless decisions—what was one more?

'I'll book a table,' he promised, touching her hair. 'What time?'

'About eight, will that suit you?'

'Mm, see you later, then.' Laura walked upstairs slowly, letting her hand trail over the varnished banister, thinking about Gino and Tom Farrell and the silver casket, lost for ever, and what a crazy day it had been.

The telephone rang as she was stepping out of the shower. She cursed and wrapped an enormous towel around herself, then ran to answer it. It was Joss. 'So you changed your mind about him,' he chuckled in greeting.

'What? Who?' For a second her mind was blank and cold water from her hair was dripping uncomfortably down her back.

'Tom Farrell telephoned me this afternoon,' Joss explained patiently. 'I *thought* there was something going on between you two.'

'Oh yes—what do you think?' Laura asked breathlessly.

'Splendid opportunity, my dear, splendid! And I'm glad you didn't let your dislike of him sway your judgment,' Joss teased, sounding pleased.

'Well ... actually I've changed my mind about him—I think I like him,' Laura revealed laughingly.

'So fickle!' He went on to talk about money and contracts, and Laura, feeling more uncomfortable by the second, did not really listen. She was glad to let Joss organise the business side of her work, she would not have had a clue how to go about it herself.

After congratulating her again and promising to sort everything out, Joss rang off, and Laura dashed back into the bathroom to get dry. It was good to know that Joss was happy with her decision to take the work Tom Farrell had offered, it made it right somehow, and she squashed all her own tiny doubts about having anything at all to do with him.

Gino knocked on her door at exactly eight o'clock, his dark eyes warm as they slid over her. She had decided to wear one of her favourite dresses, a fashionable style of soft wool, in a rich cornflower blue that made her violet eyes startling in contrast, and had left her shining hair loose to fall about her slim shoulders.

'You look lovely,' he told her huskily. 'Well, this is a celebration.' Her voice was light, as she locked her door.

It was a pleasant evening. Gino made her laugh a lot and he seemed determined not to be serious, which suited Laura perfectly. If he was in love with her, she had no idea what to do, or how to cope. She had thought about it a great deal that afternoon. Her own feelings were very clear in her mind, after a lot of heartsearching. She was very, very fond of him and valued his friendship more than anyone else's, but she did not love him. She could not bear to hurt him, though, and the only solution she had come up with was extreme—to leave the flat and not see him again. It was a totally unsatisfactory idea and one that she was loath to put into practice.

If she went away with Grace to the country for a couple of weeks, that might help her put the situation into perspective, and allow a breathing space for both Gino and herself. She was confused and lost and rather sad, because whatever the outcome she felt sure that something pure and special would be damaged beyond repair.

After the meal they strolled along the bank of the Thames, hand in hand, talking and staring into the dark, dirty water. It was a warm clear evening and there was a close harmony between them. When they got home Laura offered coffee and brandy, but Gino refused, telling her that he was exhausted, hardly able to keep his eyes open. She knew him too well not to know that he was lying—how many other times had this happened, when she had not been looking for it—but accepted his excuse with a smile. He kissed her, his mouth warm, gentle and brief, then disappeared into his flat before she even had time to thank him for the lovely evening. Depression folded round her as she climbed the stairs and as soon as she got inside, she went drearily to bed.

The next morning was spent in a flurry of activity. Laura did not wake until late and after a quick breakfast of coffee and a slice of toast, she set about packaging up her illustrations for Grace's book and generally tidying up her work desk. The place looked as if a bomb had hit it, she realised ruefully. When she was working on something, it took all her time, attention and concentration. Everything else was pushed aside until she finished. As she sifted through the rubbish, she found two library books that she had been using for research, long overdue, a letter from a friend, dated six weeks before, that she had not yet answered, and a coffee cup under a pile of preliminary drawings, that was half-filled with an obnoxious-looking liquid—presumably it had once been coffee. It really was disgraceful, she would have to make more of an effort to be organised when she was working, she resolved sternly.

By eleven forty-five, her desk was cleared and everywhere was tidy. She placed a jar of wild flowers on the pale wooden surface next to the parcel of illustrations and stood back, well pleased with herself, smiling at the empty easels, the neat rows of ceramic jars containing brushes, pencils and crayons, orderly piles of paper and rolls of canvas. Ready to start afresh, something new and different. It was almost a ceremony when she had finished a piece of work, this ritual tidying and sorting, it seemed to be the finishing touch to the work.

She looked at the watch on her wrist and her eyes widened with horror. It was nearly twelve, and Tom Farrell would be calling for her in just over half an hour. Nerves fluttered in her stomach at the thought of seeing him again.

She pushed her hair from her face and noticed how dirty her hand was. The strenuous housework had left her grubby and hot. If she hurried, she might just have time for a quick shower before getting ready. As the cool water splashed over her, she thought about what to wear. It was another bright warm day and she finally decided on black trousers, fashionably loose in style, tighter round the ankles, and a pale silk blouse. She made her face up, angry that her fingers were trembling, then dressed. She looked good, casual yet smart and elegant enough to go anywhere, precisely the effect she had been aiming for. Brushing out her hair, she fiddled with it for nearly ten minutes, trying to decide how to wear it, and in the end time won, and she left it loose, her fingers too nervous for elaborate styling anyway. She slipped two gold bangles on to her wrist and collected her handbag and a black Chinese jacket from her wardrobe before leaving the bedroom.

There was a loud, authoritative rap on the door as she walked into the lounge. It was exactly twelve-thirty. She took a deep trembling breath and opened the door.

Tom Farrell took her breath away altogether, smiling as he saw her, a slow flash of warmth in the lean darkness of his face. 'Hello, Laura my child,' he drawled with gentle mockery. She flushed brightly, staring at him as she held open the door. He seemed to tower over her, tall and powerful and fiercely attractive in dark trousers and a superbly-tailored jacket.

'The intercom. . . .' she said stupidly, still finding it difficult to breathe properly.

'The front door was open,' he said quietly.

'Gino. He's always leaving it open, anybody could just walk in, burglars, murderers, I'm surprised we. . . .' She broke off abruptly, biting her lip. Why was she talking such rubbish?

Tom raised his dark brows. 'Aren't you going to let me in?' he enquired softly. She held wide the door and stepped back. 'I'm sorry, I. . . .'

'Laura, relax!' He put down the two parcels he had been carrying under his arm and took her shoulders, feeling the tremor that ran through her at his touch. His voice was deep and calm and he bent his head and gently kissed her forehead, as though she was a frightened child. She felt a violent urge to press herself against the hard length of his body. He stood very close to her, his strong hands still curving over the slender bones of her shoulders, so close that she could feel the clean warmth of his breath on her face when he spoke, could smell the warm male scent of his skin.

It came to her then that she wanted him very badly, a desire she had never known for any man before, new and frightening in its strength. She pulled away from him, confused by such desperate feelings.

Tom watched her, his grey eyes unreadable and perceptive as he let her put distance between them.

'I . . . I'm ready,' she faltered, hearing her own voice strangely unnatural.

'You're beautiful,' he said softly.

Laura flushed. He thought she had been fishing for compliments. 'I didn't mean——'

'I know. But you are very beautiful.' He smiled at her and picked up the two parcels he had been carrying when he arrived. 'The play,' he explained, handing her one of them. 'There's a card inside with my address and telephone number in case you run into any difficulties.'

Laura took it with shaking hands. 'Thank you.' Her eyes shone as she lifted them to his, easily telling him how much it meant to her, and his eyes followed her as she walked over to place the play very carefully on her desk, holding it as though it was fine, rare porcelain that might fall to pieces at any second.

'I'll start reading it today.'

'There's no hurry,' he said, his eyes and mouth indulgent. 'Tell me, if you find that you don't like it, will you still be able to create the illustration?.'

Laura thought for a moment, her nose wrinkled in concentration. 'Yes, I'm sure I can work with material I don't personally like. I don't know whether it would affect the final results, though. I suppose it would. I'd have more, or perhaps different enthusiasms and emotions for something I liked,' she laughed selfconsciously, aware that she was probably talking rubbish again. 'Anyway, I will like your play,' she finished earnestly.

'How do you know?' Tom was staring at her again and she had the feeling that his whole attention was focused on her, behind those smoky grey eyes. It was a devastating thought.

'I read one of your plays the other day. It was beautiful, it made me cry.'

Tom smiled as she told him the title. 'Perhaps that was the idea,' he said wryly. 'Why did you read it?'

Laura shrugged. 'I was intrigued. I'd met you and I wondered what your work was like,' she said honestly.

'And whether I was really the ogre I appear to be?' he added amusedly.

'Yes, something like that,' she laughed, wondering

how she could be so transparent to him.

'And what did you decide?' His low voice shivered down her spine, and she could not tell whether or not he was serious.

'That you're not as bad as I thought you were.' It sounded *dreadful*, not the way she had meant it at all, and she coloured, her hand flying to her mouth in a charming, child-like gesture. 'Oh! I'm sorry. . . .'

Tom laughed, throwing back his dark head. 'Don't say anything else—your compliments are pretty hard to take,' he said, smiling.

Laura smiled too, although she felt dreadfully embarrassed and very gauche. What on earth had possessed her to be so blunt? When she dared to look up at him again she saw that he was holding the other parcel in his hands, and in his eyes, she saw something almost like—*hesitation*? Surely not. Tom Farrell had more self-assurance, more self-confidence than anyone she had ever met before. The very idea of any hesitation in him was totally incongruous. Yet the impression remained with her.

'This is for you,' he said, and the amusement was gone, he was cool and remote again. 'I hope you'll accept it.'

She took it from him warily, with no idea of what it could be. It was heavy, solid beneath the brown paper wrapping. 'Shall I open it now?' she asked, unsure, and he nodded silently.

She tore off the paper, her hands clumsy and nervous, then uttered a small cry of pure shock and pure delight as she saw the silver casket from the antique shop. The paper dropped to the floor unnoticed, the silver cold, smooth and shining beneath her fingers. She had thought it irrevocably lost to her, it was like a dream, and she felt dazed, hypnotised by the vivid enamels, the glowing stones, touching, looking, until she was almost dizzy. Then the fairytale faded and common sense returned. She could not possibly accept it, it was too valuable, too precious and Tom Farrell was a married man whom she hardly knew. Impossible. 'No,' she said huskily. Then again, stronger, 'No, I can't take this.' Her fingers curled around the smooth corners of the box, very tightly, as she spoke. She sensed the impatience behind his expressionless face.

'Of course you can,' he told her coolly. 'There are absolutely no strings attached and it's already precious to you. You hold it as though you can't bear to let it go.'

'But I must!' Her voice was high as she thrust the box towards him. 'Please, Tom, take it back. I can't accept it, I really can't. Please!' She cursed the tears that were filling her eyes and making her voice so high and shaky.

He did not move, his hands hanging loosely at his sides, making no effort to do as she begged, and take back the casket. 'You're being ridiculous,' he said coolly, and seeing her flinch at his hard words, said gently, 'Laura, listen to me. I saw the way you looked at that casket in the shop window, wistful and longing, you wanted it badly. I bought it for you because I think it belongs to you, and your objections have nothing to do with the casket itself, they're to do with money. There is no other way I can think of to give it to you, and personally I don't give a damn about the money. It's a gift, simple, unemotional, straightforward, so why should it worry you so much?'

She listened to what he said and had to admit that it made sense. But even so, there was something wrong in him giving her such an expensive gift. 'It's not only the money, although that *is* important, it's the fact that you're married,' she said bluntly, miserably.

His face tightened, his eyes becoming blank, shuttered. 'And you know all about my marriage, do you?' he queried coldly.

Laura flushed, hurt and guilty that she *had* listened to the gossip about him.

'I've heard——'

He did not let her finish what she intended to be an apology. 'I have no desire to know what you've heard, so you can spare me the details. I'm going to tell you something now, and whether or not you believe it is up to you.' His expression told her that he did not care one way or the other. 'My marriage is over, I haven't lived with my wife for sixteen years. Does that soothe your outraged sense of morality, I wonder?' His eyes were as hard and as cold as ice, as they flicked over her. 'You can do what the hell you like with that casket, I don't want it, and I think it would be better for both of us if we skip lunch.'

He turned away and left the flat, shutting the door very quietly behind him, leaving Laura still and silent and utterly desolate.

CHAPTER FOUR

LAURA had nightmares that night, so vivid and fearful that they woke her violently, more than once, so that she sat up and stared into the darkness of her room, heart pounding. Her thoughts were filled with Tom Farrell, his play sat untouched on her desk, accusing her somehow. She had insulted him by insinuating that he, a married man, was trying to buy her, to bribe her into his bed. She had given the impression that she saw him as immoral, unprincipled and very definitely not to be trusted. It still made her flinch inwardly when she remembered the ice in his eyes, the anger twisting his mouth.

He was a man who did not live by conventions, whereas Laura had been brought up in a strictly conventional home and it was difficult to shake off her inbred attitudes. It had meant nothing to Tom Farrell to buy the silver casket for her. She had wanted it, he had thought she should have it, and that had been his only motive. She had behaved like an outraged Victorian maiden, overreacting, choosing her words unwisely, when a compromise could have been reached. If only she'd acted sensibly!

She sighed, her thoughts turning to what he had told her about his marriage. If, as he said, he had not lived with his wife for sixteen years, then the question that haunted her raised its head—why were they not divorced? And where did Amanda Delvaux fit into the picture, into his life? But it was useless to let herself run round in circles when she did not know the facts, so she savagely punched her pillows and lay back, hoping that sleep would soon stop her thinking and give her some relief.

The following afternoon Grace arrived with Christy and Jan. Laura had invited them all to lunch a week or so before. She was in no mood for visitors after her disastrous confrontation with Tom Farrell and her subsequent restless night, but one look at Grace's washed-out paleness and her obvious depression, pushed Laura's own problems out of her mind. She gave the children pineapple juice and biscuits, and sat them in a corner with paper and crayons, then made coffee for Grace and herself.

Her friend was unusually silent as they smoked and drank coffee. 'Any news?' Laura probed gently, wondering if Grace wanted to talk.

'None. These things drag on for ever. Nick's solicitors have been in touch with mine, but it's just a case of waiting until it goes to court,' her friend replied gloomily.

Laura was silent, wishing for the thousandth time that there was something, anything, she could do to help. Grace smiled suddenly. 'Any more coffee?' She was obviously making a determined effort to pull herself together. 'Laura, I'm sorry, I know I keep apologising, but I do mean it. I never intend to be so miserable with you, I'm afraid I'm bringing everyone down at the moment.'

'Not me,' Laura said firmly, pouring out more coffee for them both. 'And besides, you can't help the way you feel and you don't have to disguise your feelings when you're with friends, so there!'

'I know, but I still feel rotten for mooching around like a wet blanket.'

Jan broke into their conversation, holding up a picture she had crayoned. 'Look what I drawed! Look, Mummy—look, Laura!'

'Drew, not drawed, darling,' Grace amended, as both girls looked at Jan's picture.

'That's your house, isn't it?' Laura said, smiling at the little child.

Jan nodded. 'Can I put it up? On there?' Her tiny hand pointed to Laura's enormous cork noticeboard.

'Of course you can, darling.' Laura fetched drawing pins from her desk and pinned up the crazily-drawn picture in the centre of the board. 'Go and draw another one, one of inside the house, and put all your toys and your favourite things in it,' she suggested, and Jan trotted back to the table, telling Christy in a loud voice what she was going to do.

'Seen anything of Tom Farrell?' Grace enquired casually, as Laura sat down.

Laura flushed, despite her efforts not to. 'I had a row with him yesterday,' she said shortly. 'And I only hope I don't see him for a very long time!' She realised that she was lying as soon as the words were spoken. She *did* want to see him, she could think of nothing else.

'Oh dear!' Grace sounded genuinely distressed. 'And I thought you two would get on so well.'

'No chance,' Laura said firmly, rather bitterly. She told Grace briefly about the illustration Tom had asked her to do, but omitted to mention the silver casket or the end of their encounter the day before. 'I'll do the work, of course, I could do with the money and it is a wonderful career opportunity, but I don't want any more to do with Tom Farrell. I shall give the work to Joss when it's finished and he can deal with him.' Why was she lying to Grace, to herself? The truth was that she was too embarrassed, too afraid of her own feelings for Tom Farrell. 'Have you thought any more about going away?' she asked, anxious to change the subject.

Grace cast her a sharp knowledgeable look. 'Actually, I might have found somewhere.' She sounded vague. 'Are you still interested in coming with me?'

'Oh yes, I definitely want to come. Where is it?' The idea of getting out of London for a while was becoming desperately important. Everything seemed to be closing in on her.

'Scotland—some place miles from civilisation.'

'Sounds terrific,' Laura said enthusiastically. 'Can you arrange it?' She wondered why Grace was being so vague. 'Who owns it? Tell me all abut it.'

Grace lit another cigarette. 'Well . . . a . . . a friend of mine has two cottages in this place—I can't remember the name. I can have the use of one for as long as I like. I was thinking of going in the next week or so, how would that suit you? I can always put it off a week if your work keeps you here.'

Laura thought about Tom Farrell's illustration. If it wasn't finished, there was no reason why she couldn't take it with her, or even leave it until she got back. He had said that there was no hurry. 'How about the weekend after this?' she suggested. 'I should have everything cleared up by then.'

'Suits me fine,' Grace smiled. 'How lovely it will be to get away from everything for a while. I'll fix up all the details and let you know. And thanks, Laura, I'm so glad you'll be coming with us. There's no reason why it shouldn't be the holiday of a lifetime!'

Her voice was excited, and Laura found that she too, felt excited at the prospect. It would be so good to get away from the city, to breathe fresh air, to see the sky.

'I hope the weather is fine, we can go for long walks, picnics, perhaps.'

Grace laughed. 'I've been warned that they have floods most years.'

'Even more of an adventure,' Laura shrugged uncaringly.

Gino arrived ten minutes later to beg some sugar and Laura invited him to stay for lunch, which delighted the children. The meal was a noisy, happy affair and Laura was glad to see Grace laughing again. The short break in Scotland would help her back on her feet, Laura was sure.

The next day she felt strong enough to read Tom Farrell's play. It took her hours to read, as had the one before, and she liked it very much. The central character was a woman, and he had written with a deep perceptive knowledge of the female sex. There was a warmth in the play, despite the sadness of the ending, a depth to the characters that had Laura living and breathing with them, while she read. And at the end, as well as tears, there was anger at the injustice done to the central character, by circumstances, by people. Laura felt dazed, when she finally put it down, stunned by the power, the compassion of the play. Ideas for her illustration formed easily in her mind and she instinctively knew, as Tom had said she would, the right thing to do, the exact picture she wanted, but the ideas were pushed aside by thoughts of the man who had written the play. She wanted to know him better, know his friendship, his love.

She shivered despite the warmth of the room and grabbed a sketching pad and pencil, her fingers flying over the paper as she captured her elusive ideas. It was easy, instinctive, almost perfect, yet she felt strangely exhausted by the time she finished. She made an omelette for her lunch, but the mere smell of it made her feel sick, and her appetite faded, and she pushed it round her plate until she could not bear to look at it and had to throw it away. She paced the room restlessly, not understanding her lightning moods of the past week, and finally, in desperation grabbed her jacket and decided to go for a walk in an effort to work off some of her energy.

There was music coming from Gino's flat and she paused for a second as she reached the bottom of the stairs, wanting to go and talk to him, to ask him to walk with her. But he was another of her problems, and more than anything she did not want to hurt him, so she walked past and out of the main door alone.

She strolled down the warm, dusty street, intending to go the park, the nearest spot of green in a sea of dirt and bricks, she thought wearily. It was quite a long walk and when she got there, she stood by the small lake for a while, staring into the brown water, before seating herself on one of the iron benches. It looked as though it was going to rain. Her eyes watched the ducks and geese on the lake, her mind full of vague unformed thoughts. She was aware that somebody came and sat beside her, but she did not look round until a low voice said, 'Hello, Laura.' Her head jerked round then, her eyes meeting the steady, impenetrable gaze of Tom Farrell. She turned away just as quickly, not answering, hating the leaping of her pulses, the hot flush of colour to her cheeks. She heard the faint click of his lighter.

'Cigarette?'he queried, and she knew that he was staring at her.

'No, thank you,' she replied shortly, gazing straight ahead of her. The faint smell of the French tobacco he smoked drifted around her. Shd did not want to talk to him, and in one swift movement she got to her feet, intending to walk away. But Tom moved just as quickly, his hand closing round her arm, pulling her gently down beside him again.

'What do you think you're doing?' she demanded breathlessly. 'Let me go!' For a moment she stared at him, taking in the hard bones of his face, the firm line of his mouth, the hooded eyes, and a peculiar weakness flooded her lower limbs.

He smiled at her. 'We've been through all this before, as I recall.'

'Tom, please. . . .' She did not know what she was begging for. He released her arm, his fingers touching her face, tracing the delicate, sensitive line of her jaw. 'I owe you an apology for the other day. I was ill-mannered, abrupt, bloody-minded. I'm sorry,' he said softly.

'It doesn't matter,' Laura put in quickly, his touch disturbing her.

'Oh, but it does, little one, and I want you to forgive me.'

She smiled at him and his eyes darkened disturbingly. 'I . . . I read your play,' she said, wanting something to talk about. Tom was silent, so she continued, 'I liked it very much. Why is it so sad?'

'Life is sad, don't you know that yet?' There was a faint harshness to his voice, his words double-edged.

'I prefer happy endings,' she said seriously.

That made him smile. 'So do I.' It was starting to rain, slow heavy droplets of water. 'Have you eaten?' he asked, staring into the dark sky.

'Not really. I made an omelette, but I couldn't eat it.'

'Eat with me,' he offered, with a brief hard smile.

'Yes, I'd like that,' she admitted shyly.

He got to his feet, stretching lazily, drawing Laura's

eyes to the powerful lines of his body, the width of his shoulders, the lean strength of his hips.

He held out his hand to her and she stood up, their glances locking in a fierce explosion of awareness. Tom saw the hunger in her eyes, and his own narrowed, flaring with light. They stared at each other.

'Laura.' Her name came from deep in his throat. She put out her hands as if to ward him off, but he moved towards her, taking her into his arms, her hands crushed flat against the hard wall of his chest, his heart beating deeply and steadily beneath her fingers. His mouth touched hers, parting her lips to his touch, kissing her deeply, hungrily, until she was weak, her body softly yielding against his.

The rain was heavy now, falling into their faces as their mouths moved hungrily together. Tom raised his head reluctantly, his eyes dark, very serious until he smiled, his fingers tenderly wiping the rain from her small face. 'You're soaked,' he teased softly.

Laura reached up and touched her hair, her fingers came away dripping. 'So I am.' Then she laughed, high pure laughter that she realised was born of sheer happiness. Everything was right again between Tom and herself, her restless miserable mood gone.

They walked to his car, hand in hand. 'You ought to change before we have lunch or you'll probably catch pneumonia,' he said, turning to her in the car, his voice possessive.

'I've got a better idea,' she said, her eyes bright and luminous on his face.

'Which is?'

'Do you like eggs?' He nodded, the line of his mouth warm and indulgent. 'I could make another omelette, perhaps more palatable than the last, and you could share it,' she suggested shyly. It was the first invitation she had ever made to him.

'Sounds fine. I'll buy some wine on the way back.' He smiled and switched on the engine, the powerful car roaring into life immediately.

'With an omelette?' she asked laughingly, relaxing back against the soft leather upholstery.

His wide shoulders lifted in a careless indolent shrug. 'Why not?'

Gino was just leaving as they arrived, and his eyes hardened as they slid to Laura's hand in Tom's. 'Work?' she asked, with a sympathetic smile.

He rolled his eyes. 'What else?'

His voice was so expressive that she laughed, and felt Tom's fingers tightening almost imperceptibly on her own. She introduced the two men, apologising again for her rudeness when last they met. Her eyes were on Gino as they talked. The hardness was gone from his eyes, he was his bright, usual self again. Tom was polite, charming and honestly admiring about Gino's mural in the hall.

They chatted for about five minutes or so, then Gino glanced at his watch. 'I have to run, I have a meeting at two-thirty. Oh, by the way Laura, Joss rang, couldn't get through to you, so he left a message with me. He's flying to Rome this afternoon, so you won't be able to reach him for three weeks. If you finish the illustration before then, deliver it directly to Tom.'

'Okay. I'll see you later,' Laura promised as he went towards his car.

'Yes, see you later, baby. 'Bye, Tom.' The car seemed to have shot down the road before he had finished speaking.

She glanced at Tom as they climbed the stairs together. There was an air of still anger about him, his face hard, closed. 'Are you angry about something?' she asked directly.

'He's a fool,' came the harsh reply.

Laura was taken aback. 'Gino? No, he's not a fool, he's a good man, a brilliant artist,' she told him earnestly.

Tom's mouth twisted cynically. 'And as a lover?'

'I don't know,' she replied with dignity. 'And do you really think I'd tell you if I did?' Her violet eyes flashed anger at him, shock.

He stared at her for a moment. 'God, I'm sorry,' he said heavily. 'An unworthy remark. Perhaps I see myself mirrored in his eyes when he looks at you.'

'What does that mean?' She was nonplussed.

'Work it out,' he suggested, his mouth compressing wryly.

She shook her head, totally confused, and opened the door to her flat.

'Go and change,' he told her, as soon as they were inside.

'Can I get you a towel or anything?' she asked, ignoring his order.

He shook his head, the light gleaming off his wet hair. 'Shall I make some coffee? A hot drink would do you good.'

'That would be nice. The kitchen's through there,' she said, staring at him in surprise. 'but I'm not an invalid you know.'

His answering smile made her heart turn over. 'Perhaps I want to look after you,' he suggested softly, mocking her, she was sure.

'I don't believe that for a second,' she retorted, but she felt the colour rising in her cheeks and fled to the bedroom without waiting for any reply.

She slipped out of her wet clothes and pulled on denim jeans and a thick baggy sweater in blue and green, tugging a brush through her damp hair and tying it back in a ponytail to dry. She could smell the delicious aroma of freshly-brewed coffee wafting through the flat as she paused in front of the long mirror near her dressing table. She frowned at her reflection, wondering if she ought to put on some make-up, but then shrugged fatalistically. Her hands were not very steady, and there was a sweet excitement churning in her stomach at the thought of having lunch with Tom Farrell. It would probably take her half an hour to apply it properly anyway.

She wandered into the lounge, on silent bare feet. Tom was standing at the window, smoking idly, staring out at the deep, dark sky and the rain. Laura stared at his powerful physique, his proud black head, in silence, until he must have sensed her presence, because he turned slowly, his grey eyes sliding over her assessingly.

'Can . . . can I have some coffee?' she faltered, dry-mouthed suddenly.

He indicated a chair. 'Sit down and I'll pour some for you.'

She did as she was told, curling her feet beneath her on the scarlet sofa, as he poured the coffee. She watched his hands, so very strong, lean and brown. Closing her eyes, she could imagine him touching her, caressing her, and a small sigh escaped her. Dangerous, crazy thoughts that she pushed firmly out of her mind. As she drank her coffee, she could not help watching him covertly from beneath her lashes. He seemed totally relaxed, his hard face blank, unreadable, grey eyes hooded, hiding any expression.

He looked at her, noting her tiny nervous movements, the tension in the vulnerable line of her mouth. 'Tell me about yourself,' he said gently, breaking the silence, trying to put her at ease.

'I don't think there's anything worth telling—no big adventures, no dramas,' Laura replied with a slightly selfconscious smile.

'Ah, but you wouldn't know, would you?' he said, with a slight expressive movement of his hands. 'Tell me about your family, your childhood.'

So Laura told him about her parents, now living in New York, and about Nancy and her husband, and then about the childhood that she remembered as fairly happy and fairly stable, surprised that it interested him. He listened carefully, his eyes intent as he learned about her.

When she could think of no more to say about herself, she said, 'It must be your turn now. Do you have any brothers or sisters?'

'I have a brother, but I've no idea who he is or where he is, he may even be dead for all I know.' There was no emotion at all in his face. Laura stared at him in amazement, her heart stirring with compassion, despite the remote tone of his voice.

'But . . . but why?'

'We were split up when we were kids, I haven't seen him since I was four years old. I tried to trace him, but he seems to have disappeared off the face of the earth after the age of twenty-five,' Tom replied levelly, almost without interest.

'And what about your parents?'

'My father walked out on us just after I was born and my mother turned to drink. A few years later she was an alcoholic, totally incapable of looking after herself, let alone two kids, so my brother and I were taken off her and for some reason, put into separate homes. She died when I was eight.' He was brief and expressionless.

'God, that's awful! I'm so sorry,' Laura whispered, shocked by the brutality of his childhood.

'Don't be,' he told her indifferently. 'It was years ago, I hardly remember her.'

Laura was silent. She wanted to ask more questions, find out more about him, but she sensed that he did not really want to talk about it. She tried to picture him as a child, but found that she couldn't. Perhaps mentally he had never been a child, the harsh, callous and difficult life had made him old before his time. Her heart ached for the boy he had been, but one look at the man told her that he would not take pity or compassion. He was hard and tough and supremely confident, with a mind that could dissect other people's motives very easily. Any show of sympathy, totally unnecessary, totally unneeded, would be shot down in flames, mocked by that razor-sharp brain.

Tom drained his coffee in one swift mouthful and smiled at her teasingly. 'Was it my imagination or did you offer me half an omelette when we were in the car?'

She jumped to her feet. 'I'll start it right away,' she laughed, walking into the kitchen.

He followed, loose-limbed, graceful and silent. 'Can I help?' He was leaning back against the wooden cupboards, indolently folding his arms across his chest, and Laura shook her head nervously.

'No, I don't think so. Omelettes are so easy, even I can make them without any help.'

He watched her while she worked, watched the unselfconscious grace of her body as she moved about the room. She felt those cool grey eyes on her as she chopped mushrooms and onions and grated cheese, the fierce pull of his attraction disturbing her deeply, making her hands clumsy, unsteady. A fork clattered from her fingers, noisy and betraying.

'Please don't watch me, it makes me nervous,' she said desperately over her shoulder, not meeting his eyes but concentrating on keeping her voice steady.

Tom walked towards her, his hands closing gently on her shoulders, turning her towards him. His eyes searched her delicate face and she found herself looking up at him, drawn by his dark intense gaze. Her heartbeat accelerated wildly.

'You're not still afraid of me, are you?' he asked softly.

'Sometimes.' She was honest.

He raised his eyebrows, surprised. 'Shall I set the table?'

The complete change of subject floored her. 'Yes, if you like,' she answered vaguely.

'It won't take my mind off you—my eyes, yes, but not my mind,' he warned with a teasing smile.

'You're impossible!' She couldn't help laughing.

'And you're not nervous any more,' he said, releasing her.

'No.' She turned back to the eggs, feeling madly happy and, as he said, not at all nervous.

Her omelette was perfect, light and delicious, and she prepared a salad to accompany it and cut up a crusty french loaf. The wine that Tom had bought was light and dry and rather intoxicating, and by the time they had finished the meal, Laura was replete and rather flushed, her eyes brilliant and drowsy in her small face.

'Fantastic omelette,' Tom commented, leaning back in his seat and reaching for his cigarettes.

'Thank you.' She smiled at him and accepted a cigarette, feeling wonderfully content in his company.

Over coffee he urged her to talk about herself again,

asking questions about her work, her life, and she found herself telling him almost everything, all her hopes and dreams and fears, until she realised that he probably knew more about her than she did herself. And in her lazy, golden mood that did not matter at all, she had a secret feeling that he could read her mind anyway.

She told him that she had done some preliminary sketches for his illustration and asked if he would like to see them, but he refused, telling her that he only wanted to see the finished result, it was her creation until then, secret, growing, developing into something perfect. Laura had not thought of it like that before, but as she did, she agreed with him and was happy that he had such confidence in her.

Tom insisted on washing up, leaving Laura curled up on a chair, staring out of the window. The afternoon was very dark, rain still lashing down outside with no sign of letting up. It was the sort of afternoon that made one happy to be indoors, she thought lazily, listening to Tom whistling as he worked in the kitchen. She got to her feet and padded out to the kitchen, leaning against the door jamb, watching him as he had watched her before the meal. She felt a little lightheaded, not drunk at all, but contented, calm and happy.

'I'm not used to drinking at lunchtime,' she told him.

'Two glasses of wine is hardly drinking,' he replied with dry indulgence.

'It is for me.'

Suddenly he stood in front of her, staring down at her. 'Laura, we'll have to talk soon, about you and me.' His voice was serious, with a deep brooding edge to it.

She did not understand. 'What is there to talk about?' she asked, feeling a sharp spasm of worry tightening her stomach.

Tom raised his dark brows. 'Don't you know?'

'I don't want to know,' she said faintly, panicking now. Thoughts raced round her head. Was he talking about his marriage? She could not bear it.

'Laura. . . .'

'No, I don't want to talk,' she cut in quickly, moving forward so that she was almost touching him. 'Hold me,' she whispered, her eyes filling with unexpected tears.

She heard him murmur her name again as he took her into his arms, moulding her tightly to the hard length of his body. She relaxed against him, terribly afraid that she would not see him again after today. That must be what he wanted to talk about, and the thought hurt her more than she would have thought possible. She pressed herself closer to him and heard him draw breath unsteadily, his arms tightening. His strength seemed to weaken her, her legs turning to jelly as she lifted her head and stared into his face, her lips parted, unknowingly provocative. Tom's eyes were dark, glittering, his fingers trailing gently across the white skin of her throat.

'You look like a child with your hair back like that,' he murmured huskily. 'A sweet, desirable child. Your skin is like a child's too, so soft, so white em—you're beautiful.'

He lowered his head, his mouth touching hers gently. Laura could not help her response. His mouth was warm, firm and beautiful, triggering sensations deep inside her, and her lips moved instinctively beneath his. His kiss deepened, hungry, passionate, feeding on her response, exploring the sweetness of her mouth.

Her arms crept around his neck, her fingers stroking through his hair, touching the heavy muscles of his shoulders, her heart beginning to pound deeply, languorously. Then his arms slid beneath her and he was carrying her effortlessly out of the kitchen into the lounge, laying her down gently on the scarlet sofa, his hands releasing the ribbon that held her hair, threading his fingers through the heavy golden silk. He came down beside her, his mouth parting hers again with hungry expertise, kissing her long and deeply until she could think of nothing but the pleasure of his mouth, the strength of his body. She moaned softly as his hand slid beneath the heavy woollen sweater to stroke and caress the soft bare skin of her waist. He was trembling, his lips at her throat, at the tiny pulse that thundered beneath her thin skin. Laura touched his hair, his shoulders, his broad chest. But it was not enough. She wanted to touch his skin, fumbling with the buttons of his shirt until it was open, revealing the hard lines of his chest and the rough dark hair that covered it, arrowing up from the flat planes of his stomach.

Desire swept through her, turning the blood in her veins to fire, heating, running swiftly, as she looked at him. She touched him tentatively. His skin was warm and smooth over tense unyielding muscles. 'Laura. . . .' His voice was thick, as he caught her hands, stilling them against his body. He took a long deep breath and released her, moving away with swift grace, off the sofa, to light two cigarettes, passing one to her, his eyes burning on her for a second. She watched him draw deeply on his cigarette, expelling the smoke in a long stream through his nostrils. His shirt still hung open, his powerful body tense and very still. She felt weak, aching and confused.

'Tom. . . .' She spoke his name pleadingly, wanting to ask why he had rejected her, but not knowing how to. He *did* want her, his mouth and hands had told her that in no uncertain terms.

He turned and stared down at her, at her huge, pleading eyes, at the bruised softness of her mouth and the tousled silk of her hair. 'Don't look at me like that,' he groaned huskily. 'You don't know what it does to me.'

'I'm not a child, Tom, I know exactly what I'm doing,' she said, with a sweet, strangely innocent smile.

He sighed heavily. 'No, you don't.' His hands clenched into fists by his sides. 'I have to go,' he muttered harshly.

Laura stared at him, her eyes inviting. 'Please . . . don't go,' she whispered, too trapped in the forceful web of her own aroused emotions to be able to think straight.

Tom swore under his breath. 'Laura, don't make it any harder for me than it is already. Dear God, do you think I want to leave you? Believe me, I don't, but I must go.'

She turned her face away from him, terribly hurt, still aching with desire for him. He was angry and she did not know why, and she suddenly felt the wet warmth of tears on her face, tears she had not even noticed falling.

Tom came to her then, crouching down beside her, tilting her face up to his. 'Don't cry, Laura,' he said gently. 'None of it's worth crying over.'

She stared at him, misunderstanding what he was saying. 'Maybe not to you,' she retorted tremulously, scrubbing the back of her hand across her wet face.

His eyes softened. 'I want you, Laura, more than

I've ever wanted any woman in my life, but if I made love to you now, you would hate me afterwards,' he said quietly. 'And I couldn't take that.'

'How do you know?' she hiccoughed, transfixed by the tenderness she saw in his face.

'Because you don't want an affair, you told me that, and I have nothing else to offer you,' he said bitterly. 'Your innocence destroys me, I find that I can't take it.'

His words had a deep effect on her, stiffening her spine, instantly dissolving the heated desire firing her body. She had offered him everything and he had refused in the cruellest possible way, by reminding her that he was not free. She felt embarrassed and humiliated, crossing that thin line between love—and she realised in that split second that she *did* love him—and hatred. Defensive anger rose in her and she hated herself as much as she hated him. What had possessed her to become involved with him? He was married, and although he had told her that he was separated from his wife, he had not divorced her, which seemed to indicate that he had no desire to be free.

Her imagination ran wild. Perhaps there was more to the marriage than anybody outside it knew. And if there was, what did that make her? She flayed herself with the cruel, cold names that described a woman who broke up another woman's marriage. She felt sick and terribly weary, wanting to lash out at Tom, because he had hurt her and because it was partly his fault too. He had pursued her, forcing his company on her when all she had wanted was to try and forget him. Now it was too late to forget, she had fallen deeply and irrevocably in love with him, he would remain in her heart until she died. How can I love him? she asked herself desperately. How?

'Feeling guilty about your wife?' she enquired coldly, sitting up and pushing away his hands.

The tenderness faded from his eyes and they became curiously blank. 'You little bitch,' he said expressionlessly. 'Are you?'

'I don't have to,' she retorted icily, aiming to hurt. 'She's not my problem.'

Tom stood up slowly, buttoning his shirt, tucking it into his jeans with lithe, easy movements that drew her eyes despite her dislike of him at that moment, 'No,' he agreed coolly. 'Your problem seems to be frustration and a decided lack of good sense.'

Outraged colour lit Laura's face. 'Oh, you swine!' she choked, jumping to her feet, her hand moving up as fast as lightning, to slap the cold arrogance from his face. But he was too quick for her, his long fingers easily catching her wrist, their grip cruel and bruising as he twisted her hand away.

'I advise you not to try that again,' he warned quietly, and for the first time Laura felt frightened of him, of his strength, of the blank iciness in his grey eyes.

'You wouldn't believe how much I dislike you,' she said vehemently. 'I wish I'd never met you!' The truth of her words burned in the violet depths of her eyes and she saw his face tauten, as though she really had hit him.

He released her wrist abruptly and turned away, moving to the window. 'I didn't get that impression when I had you in my arms just now, when you begged me not to leave. You would have given me everything, gladly,' he said harshly.

Laura flinched. 'Which only means that you're an expert when it comes to making love. Congratulations—you can make me respond to you physically. It certainly doesn't make me like you any more. It only makes me hate myself.' His body stiffened and he did not reply, but walked towards the door. He seemed calm, very controlled, very cold. 'Yes!' she shouted in frustration at the broad, unyielding sweep of his back. 'Go, and please don't come here again!'

Tom turned as he reached the door, his eyes flicking over her, deadly and contemptuous. His mouth was tight and very angry. He seemed about to say something.

'Go away!' Laura repeated desperately, before he had the chance, knowing a fierce, treacherous longing to go to him, to feel the hard warmth of his body again, the hungry touch of his mouth.

He stared at her for a moment longer, then walked out of the room and her life, in hard, icy silence.

CHAPTER FIVE

AFTER he had gone Laura sat for hours, still and alone, exactly where Tom had left her. So this was the end, she thought with dull weariness. It was such a short time since she had met him. He had changed her life, yet he had walked away from their brief time together unscathed, while she had fallen in love for the first time, the only time in her life. She had the dreadful feeling that she would never love anybody else. There was a hard heavy lump of pain like a stone in her chest, but she could not cry to release it. She closed her eyes, aching with longing for him, and thought about the cruel, unjust things she had said to him. He was right, of course, too perceptive by half. She *had* been frustrated, hurt by his sudden withdrawal, shocked to the core by the realisation that she was in love, so unsure of herself and of him, fighting the feelings she had never before experienced. And when she thought about it objectively she knew he was not to blame.

Laura ran her fingers through her hair in numb despair. She had told Tom she did not want an affair with him, then had acted like a spoiled child when he had accepted her terms. It was not easy and certainly not very pleasant to face the fact that she was in the wrong, all the way down the line, but shrugging fatalistically, she knew that motive and blame did not matter any more, Tom hated her now, the damage was done and nothing could change that, not even her love for him.

Love. How could it have happened? How could it,

when she had been so determined, fighting it every inch of the way? She had been so very careful all these years, desperate not to repeat her mistakes, yet within a few days all her barriers had been shattered beyond repair.

When she thought about those months just after her seventeenth birthday, and she did her best not to, she could still remember her feelings with intense clarity. She had been so young, so very sensitive and innocent, her adult personality barely formed, at a key turning point in her life. Of course it didn't hurt now, it hadn't for years. It hadn't even been love, but at the time it had changed her life, stamped her personality for ever.

She could still remember his face, laughing. He had always been laughing, nothing had bothered him. Laura had been spending the summer with her cousin on her uncle's farm in the Lake District, and Ryan had been a casual summer worker, a drifter. She had been fascinated by him, believing herself in love, her feelings fired more by her imagination than by reality.

He told her she was beautiful, he talked to her, laughed with her, and she believed everything he said, never having met anybody like him before. Much older, more experienced and somehow romantic, Laura had idolised him right up to that last terrible evening, certain that he must care for her as she cared for him.

All these years later, she could still hardly bear to think about it. She still remembered the high dim barn, the rough sharpness of the sweetly smelling hay and Ryan's eyes, not laughing any more but hard and cruel and intent.

He had called her a tease and much worse when she resisted him. Her fear had been mingled with bewilderment and a destructive disillusioning, as she struggled, screaming. Her uncle and the farm manager, hearing her stifled screams, had rushed in, pulling Ryan violently away from her. So lucky that they had been within earshot, if they hadn't have been. . . .

She had returned to London the following day almost a different girl, solitary, withdrawn, suspicious. That one summer, such a formative time in her developement, had changed her life, she had felt unable to trust her own judgment of people.

She had always been shy, quiet by nature, but that one horrifying incident, while not damaging her permanently, had severely shaken her self-confidence. She found it difficult to trust people, particularly men, and found it almost impossible to form close relationships, her kindness and warmth suppressed beneath a barrier of ice that Tom Farrell had managed to crack wide open without even trying, it seemed.

That was why she had treated him with such hostility, such cruelty, she realised. She was rawly exposed to the world again, and it hurt, and however wrong, it was all too easy to blame Tom, as she had been doing.

She covered her face with her hands, seeing herself very clearly for the first time in years. Her deliberately-chosen lonely, solitary life had protected her well, yet at the same time had stifled and restricted the natural growth of her personality. She could see that now the shell was broken. It was going to be a difficult time for her, she was alive again—yes, her pain told her that, but her deep mistrust still lingered. She had lost Tom, the one person she had begun to trust, and she had no idea what to do.

So she sat alone as darkness fell.

Gino knocked on her door just before seven, but she did not answer; she could not face anybody. Finally she got to her feet, her whole body stiff and aching, and picking up Tom's play, went to bed, feeling worse than she had ever done before in her life.

It was no better the next morning; she felt just as miserable, just as lonely. She wondered whether or not he would still want her to illustrate his play. It did not really matter, she would do the illustration and leave the decision to him. She read bits of the play over and over again, carrying it round the flat with her. In the end, of course, she had to make an effort and pull herself together, shower and do the shopping and housework.

Grace rang just before lunch, sounding excited. 'It's all fixed!' she announced, immediately Laura picked up the reciever.

'Great!' Laura tried to inject some enthusiasm into her voice.

'Are you all set for next weekend, then?'

Laura bit her lower lip, arriving at a sudden decision. 'We could go sooner if you like,' she suggested casually.

'How about Tuesday or Wednesday?' There was a pause on the other end of the line. 'Laura, is everything all right?' Grace asked concernedly.

'Yes, of course it is.' Laura almost smiled at her grim determination to sound normal.

Grace was not convinced, she could tell, but she didn't push it, merely saying, 'The sooner the better for me, you know that.'

'Shall we say Wednesday definitely?' Laura was anxious for something definite, some sort of rock that she could hold on to.

'Yes, Wednesday suits me fine,' Grace replied. 'So shall we make the arrangements now?'

It was decided that they would travel up to Scotland in Grace's car, and take a small amount of food with them, just in case there was any difficulty obtaining provisions.

'Right, I'll pick you up at ten o'clock on Wednesday morning. Be ready,' Grace instructed crisply, when everything was finally worked out. 'By the way, how's your work for Tom Farrell going?'

'I haven't started it really,' Laura said vaguely.

'Are you getting on with him any better?'

Why was Grace persisting in talking about the one man she could not even bear to think about? Laura wondered tiredly. 'No. I don't want to talk about Tom Farrell,' she answered unsteadily, unable to hide her pain at even having to mention his name.

'Oh, Laura, I'm sorry. . . .'

'I'm sorry too. Er . . . look, I have to go. I'll see you on Wednesday.' She hung up quickly, tears pouring suddenly and uncontrollably down her face. She knew that she had been rather rude, but she also knew that Grace would understand—she hoped so, anyway.

During the next four days, she did nothing but work on Tom's illustration. She worked all day and late into the night on it, wanting to finish it, but unable to rush it. And while she worked, she read the play constantly, until she knew whole passages of it off by heart. The frontispiece illustration developed as she worked on it, as she understood more of the play, into something so brilliant that she could hardly believe it was her own work. She had never been so involved before in a commission, and the results were staggering, the best piece of work she had ever produced, superbly drafted, sensitive and emotional in content.

When at last on that fourth day the final brush stroke was done, she sat back in her chair, terribly tired, emotionally drained, but very, very satisfied. She lifted the picture on to a display board and stared at it. Yes, she decided contentedly, it was the most difficult, the most perfect piece of work she had ever done. So this was job satisfaction.

The work had been an anaesthetic, now wearing off with its completion, all the pain, misery and memories crowding in, new and raw. Luckily she was too exhausted, both mentally and physically for them to hurt as they should have. She stumbled to her feet, her eyes aching, and peered at her watch. It was ten o'clock and she was dead on her feet. She made some tea with numb, clumsy hands, then fell into bed and slept for fourteen hours.

The next morning, when at last she woke, she felt refreshed and almost happy in a dull kind of way. The hard miserable band of pain around her heart was still there and thoughts of Tom would not leave her mind, but the fact that she had finished the illustration made her actually *smile* as she jumped out of bed. It was a bright sunny day, a perfect day for re-establishing contact with the outside world. She had no idea what was going on, she realised. She had not read a paper, listened to the radio or television or even answered the telephone or the door while she had been working. She had been completely isolated in her involvement with the play, living in a different world.

She took a bath instead of her usual quick shower, revelling in the hot scented water, then washed and dried her hair and dressed in chocolate brown velvet slacks and a matching silk blouse. She stared at herself in the mirror as she applied her make-up. Her eyes had faint dark smudges beneath them, her mouth was somehow mysterious, vulnerable. She shrugged and went downstairs to see Gino, hoping he would give her breakfast, as she could not find so much as a stale crust in her own kitchen.

He was working at his desk, swearing under his

breath and screwing up sheets of paper, flinging them moodily into the waste basket.

'Am I interrupting?' Laura asked, sticking her head round the door, after receiving no answer to her knock.

His thin face lit up with a warm smile. 'Never! In fact you've probably saved my life. If I carry on much longer I'm going to go insane! Come in.'

'Actually I'm on the scrounge,' she admitted wryly. 'Any chance of some breakfast? My cupboard's utterly bare.'

'What would you like, eggs? Toast? Just name it.'

"Toast would be fine—with some coffee,' she added impishly.

'Hold on five minutes,' Gino said, disappearing into the kitchen. 'Make yourself at home.'

Laura smiled at his kindness, his brightness. 'What are you working on that's causing so much anguish?' she shouted out to him.

'Soap powder,' he called back mournfully. 'Today it does *not* inspire me.'

Laura laughed. 'You'll get there in the end.' Gino always did. He was fast making a name for himself in advertising, for being original, unusual and brilliant.

'You think so?' He reappeared, balancing a laden tray in one hand. 'Right now I feel as though I never want to *see* another packet of soap powder, let alone wax lyrical!' He set down the tray and sat down opposite her, handing her a plate of deliciously browned toast. 'Honey,' he said, indicating the jar on the tray. 'It's very good for you.'

'I can't eat all this!' There were at least four slices on the plate.

He shrugged. 'So I'll help you.' He poured out two

cups of coffee as Laura spread honey thickly on to a slice of toast.

'Lovely,' she pronounced after the first bite. 'Thank you.'

Gino smiled. 'My pleasure.' He ate a slice of toast with lightning speed then said. 'I haven't seen you for ages, where have you been?'

'Chained to my desk, working. I haven't been out for four days,' she replied with a rueful smile. 'I've been working on Tom Farrell's illustration.'

Gino stiffened imperceptibly. 'Ah. Finished it?'

She nodded. 'I'm so excited about it. It's the best thing I've ever done. It absorbed me totally, stretched my talent and my brain to the limit.' The excitement was still in her voice.

'Can I see it?'

'Mm, come up when we've finished breakfast.'

Gino poured more coffee for them both, then suddenly said, 'You deserve a night out, there's a party tonight.' He paused and Laura saw the hesitation in him. 'Fancy coming with me?' He asked so casually, yet his eyes were very serious.

'Yes, I do,' she said simply. 'What time?'

'We could go out for dinner and straight on,' he suggested with a smile.

'Okay, sounds lovely.'

When they had finished their late breakfast he followed her upstairs to see her illustration. He was the first person to see it, and she held her breath as he carefully picked it up and walked over to the window, examining it in the cold piercing daylight. She found herself still and tense, fingers childishly crossed as she waited for his comments. It was *so* important that he liked it.

'Well?' she finally prompted, impatience getting the better of her.

'It's—beautiful,' he said sincerely. 'Brilliant. I haven't read the play, so I can't say anything about that, but this picture. . . .'

'Oh, thank you!' She kissed his cheek impulsively. 'I was so afraid you wouldn't like it, scared, I suppose, in case it had all been my imagination.'

He smiled. 'Well, it's not. It's incredible, baby, and I agree, it's the best thing you've ever done.' He sighed then, catching sight of the clock on the wall. 'But I'd better get back to my soap powder.'

When he had gone Laura walked over to the window, deep in thought. The illustration was finished, which severed any contact with Tom Farrell. Her heart twisted painfully. She would probably never see him again, but there was nothing she could do about it. He did not even want an affair, she thought unjustly. The only sensible thing to do was to put him out of her mind, even if she could not put him out of her heart. The trouble was, though, that she knew it would be impossible. She turned from the window and started to pack up the illustration. She would have to deliver it to his house, the sooner the better, she supposed. Then it really would be over.

She slid it carefully into a large cardboard folder, then wrapped it in brown paper and string. It took her a while to find the card with his address on and she stared at it with sad eyes. The address was in a very expensive area of London. She brushed her hair and slipped on a jacket, then rang for a taxi. She felt tense, nervous, as she waited and lit a cigarette. Would Tom be at home? She did not think she could face him, but oh, how she longed to see him again, even from a distance.

'Tom.' She whispered his name, shocked by the rush of pure emotion that filled her. She had never *ever* believed in love at first sight. It had been a dream, albeit a nice dream, an impossible one. Now she knew it to be a reality, it had happened—she did not know how or why, but she loved Tom Farrell and it hurt. She remembered something he had said: 'Life is sad, don't you know that yet?' Well, if she hadn't then, she certainly did now.

The intercom buzzed. Her taxi had arrived. She felt close to panic as they crawled through the city, her nerves stretching tighter and tighter as they came nearer to Tom's house. At last, yet far too soon, she was paying the driver, sliding out of the taxi. 'It may never happen, darlin'!' he told her cheerfully, as he flicked on the 'For Hire' sign. Laura smiled, thinking, too late, it already has.

It was a big old house that she stood in front of. She carefully checked the address on the card, playing for time, then rang the bell, her heart beating suffocatingly fast, praying that it would not be Tom who came to the door. She did not want to see him, she thought in panic, her earlier longing dissolving in a rush of fear. Damn Joss for swanning off to Italy when she needed him! She wanted to dump the package on the step and run. There was no sign of life from within, so she rang the bell again, half hoping that it had been a wasted journey and that she would have to come back another time.

She turned away from the door and gazed down the quiet road, wondering what to do, jumping visibly when a low French, female voice behind her asked, 'Can I help you?' She spun round and saw Amanda Delvaux in the doorway, tall and beautiful in a powder blue silk negligee.

There was the faintest impatience in the Frenchwoman's eyes, as she pushed a languid hand through the tousled auburn softness of her hair. 'Can I help you?' she repeated slowly. But Laura was speechless, staring, feeling as though someone had just given her an almighty punch in the stomach.

'I . . . er. . . .' she stammered, her mouth refusing to form the words she wanted to say.

Recognition suddenly dawned in Amanda Delvaux's blue eyes. 'Ah, now I remember,' she said, her voice attractively husky. 'The restaurant. You are here to see Tom? He's. . . .'

'No, I don't want to see him,' Laura cut in, suddenly finding her tongue. 'I wonder if I could leave this for him. He'll know who it's from. It's very important,' she added desperately, as she thrust the package into Amanda Delvaux's hands. She knew exactly where Tom Farrell was—in bed, no doubt waiting for the return of his lover, this beautiful Frenchwoman.

'No message?' Amanda Delvaux asked curiously.

'No.' Laura turned away, the soft sensuous blue silk of the other woman's nightwear making her feel sick. 'If you'll just give it to him.'

'Yes, very well.' Amanda Delvaux was staring at her with open curiosity now, no doubt amazed by Laura's strange behaviour.

Laura steeled herself once more and looked into the Frenchwoman's drowsy blue eyes. 'Thank you. Goodbye,' she said quickly, almost gasping from the tearing pain at the thought that as soon as she left, this woman would be back in Tom's arms. The thought of them together, making love, tortured her and she walked away from the house as though the devil himself was after her.

She walked for hours, not feeling at all like going home, her mind whirling. Why should she be so surprised that Amanda Delvaux was his lover? After all, she had seen them together in the restaurant, on that first day, had seen the possessive touch of the Frenchwoman's hand. She had wondered at the time if they were lovers, had assumed they probably were. Now she knew for sure. It boiled down to jealousy, sheer livid green jealousy, and the realisation that Tom Farrell was nothing more than a philandering, uncaring swine, she told herself fiercely.

Presumably Amanda Delvaux had been living at his house all the time Laura had known him. She caught her thoughts short. There was another way of looking at it, of course, more objectively, without being blinded by her own vanity, her own bitterness and love. He was a man of the world, women came easily to him, like herself, wanting him a thousand times more than he wanted them. Grace had told her that. Could she really blame him for taking what was so readily offered? According to him his marriage was over, he had a beautiful French mistress and Laura was bitter because he had refused to become involved, to take advantage of the fierce, fleeting attraction that had flared between them. Fool, fool! she told herself miserably. It was not his fault that she had stupidly fallen in love with him. She was glad, in a strange, heartaching way, that she would not see him again. At least she would not be leaving herself open to humiliation, constantly taunted by her love.

They said that time healed all wounds. Would it for her? In future she would keep herself to herself. She had been right all along in her instincts. Apart from casual friendship, any relationship with a man was doomed to pain and disaster. Never again, she told herself sternly, and noticing how late it was, made her way home.

She dressed without any particular enthusiasm for

LOVE BEYOND REASON
There was a surprise in store for Amy!

Amy had thought nothing could be as perfect as the days she had shared with Vic Hoyt in New York City—before he took off for his Peace Corps assignment in Kenya.

Impulsively, Amy decided to follow. She was shocked to find Vic established in his new life... and interested in a new girl friend.

Amy faced a choice: be smart and go home... or stay and fight for the only man she would ever love.

MAN OF POWER
Sara took her role seriously

Although Sara had already planned her escape from the subservient position in which her father's death had placed her, Morgan Haldane's timely appearance had definitely made it easier.

All Morgan had asked in return was that she pose as his fiancée. He'd confessed to needing protection from his partner's wife, Louise, and th part of Sara's job proved easy

But unfortunately for Sara heart, Morgan hadn't told her about Monique...

Your Romantic Adventure Starts Here.

THE LEO MAN
"He's every bit as sexy as his father!"

Her grandmother thought that description would appeal to Rowan, but Rowan was determined to avoid any friendship with the arrogant James Fraser.

Aboard his luxury yacht, that wasn't easy. When they were all shipwrecked on a tropical island, it proved impossible.

And besides, if it weren't for James, none of them would be alive. Rowan was confused. Was it merely gratitude that she now felt for this strong and rugged man?

THE WINDS OF WINTER
She'd had so much— now she had nothin

Anne didn't dwell on it, but the pain was still with her—the double-edged pain of grief and rejection.

It had greatly altered her; Anne barely resembled the girl who four years earlier had left her husband, David. He probably wouldn't even recognize her—especially with another name.

Anne made up her mind. Sh just had to go to his house to discover if what she suspected was true...

the party that evening. It was too late to back out, even though she longed to, she could not disappoint Gino. Thank God I'll be in Scotland, away from all this the day after tomorrow, she thought, as she slid into the cool and sophisticated black dress she had chosen. Nothing to do but walk in the countryside, relax, sit by the fire at night. She fastened the clinging dress and slipped her feet into high-heeled black shoes. She left her hair loose, tumbling to her slim shoulders, and fastened three gold chains around her neck. Her make-up was perfect, she noted, without satisfaction, as she examined her appearance. She looked calm, cool and very attractive, but she did not give a damn, she was too busy trying to build a hard icy case for her aching heart.

Gino's eyes were appreciative as they sat in the restaurant. 'You look stunning,' he told her with a careful smile.

'Thanks.' She was casual, not wanting to encourage him, her eyes flicking over the menu. She did not feel very hungry.

Ordering a salad, she twisted the stem of her wine glass between her fingers and looked at Gino. He was wearing a pale grey suit, he was dark and attractive, but she felt nothing but fondness for him. She sipped her wine, toying with the idea of getting good and tight. It would dull the pain, help her through the evening.

'I forgot to tell you, Tom Farrell called this afternoon, wanting to see you,' Gino said carelessly, over dessert.

Laura's fork halted in mid-air. 'Oh? Did he say what he wanted?' she asked, striving to keep her voice uncaring, while her heart beat faster.

'To me? Are you kidding?' Gino laughed shortly. 'I got the feeling he wanted to smash my teeth in! Come to think of it, I always get that feeling when he's around.'

Laura flushed and lowered her bright head. 'I'm sorry,' she mumbled, her mind working fast. Tom must have known that she had been to the house, unless Amanda Delvaux had not given him the illustration. Was there something wrong with it? What did he want?

'For what?' Gino asked cheerfully. 'Look, Laura, I know it's none of my business, but what exactly is going on between you two?'

'Absolutely nothing,' she replied with flat honesty, her colour running higher.

She hated Gino's relief, as he said, 'Not from the want of trying on his part, I'd say. He was as mad as hell this afternoon.'

'I don't want to know,' Laura lied hurriedly. 'Where is this party?' She ignored the speculative probing gleam in his eyes, as he accepted her clumsy changing of the subject.

'Knightsbridge. Raymond Chambers is the man—more money than he knows what to do with, hence this lavish party.' Laura recognised the name, a big name in the art world.

They arrived just after ten, and the party was well under way, noisy, warm and crowded. Laura didn't particularly enjoy parties at the best of times, and as the night wore on she became more and more amazed that she had agreed to come at all. She drank whisky and ginger, danced with Gino and chatted with empty cheerfulness to people she recognised, people she was introduced to, until her head was buzzing with the effort of appearing happy.

She pushed her way through the crowd, needing some air, some peace, suddenly stopping dead in her tracks half way across the room, her whole body tensing as she stared at the tall, powerful, dark-haired man near the door. Tom Farrell.

Her pulses raced desperately fast as she looked at him, lean and strong and virile in tight jeans and a dark shirt, the clothes that revealed his total disregard for convention, for petty social rules, and despite his casual attire he was the most startling, magnificent man in the room, the female eyes watching him from all directions verifying this. He was with Amanda Delvaux, beautiful in pale green, and a man in a dark suit, who looked tanned, vaguely foreign. Tom was smiling down at the Frenchwoman, his dark head bent, attentive, the man in the suit laughing at something he said. How long had he been at the party? Why hadn't Laura noticed him before? Had he seen her? Miserably she realised that if he had, he had made no move to speak to her or even acknowledge her presence. He obviously found Amanda Delvaux even more engrossing than usual tonight, she thought spitefully.

An accidental elbow in her back brought her to her senses and she averted her eyes, moving back in a wide semi-circle to approach the door without meeting Tom face to face. Fortunately his attention was fully occupied by the two people he was talking to and he did not see her as she slipped out into the cold night air.

Laura breathed in deeply, her heart beating a little slower now. She felt hurt and sick, her head reeling from the spirit she had been drinking so recklessly and her heart aching with love for Tom, her need for him. It had been a shock to see him, so unexpected when she had accepted the fact that she would not see him again. Her mind's eye filled with the picture of him bending his proud dark head, the light gleaming on his hair, on the tanned hardness of his cheekbones, to catch Amanda Delvaux's words, his beautiful mouth slightly smiling, indulgent.

She couldn't go back inside. Her eyes filled with tears of sadness and self-pity. Why can't he love me? she wondered with weary misery. Why can't he even care for me a little when I love him so much? But even if he did care for you, a tiny cold voice in her brain told her, there would still be his wife, there would still be Amanda Delvaux.

A hand touched her shoulder lightly and she spun round, her violet eyes wide, shimmering with tears. But it was not Tom, as she had feared. It was Gino, dark eyes narrowed and concerned.

'Are you ill?' he demanded worriedly. 'I've been looking all over for you!'

Laura grasped at his words. 'I think . . . I think I've had a little too much to drink,' she replied with a shaky smile.

'Shall we leave?' he asked gently.

'I don't want to drag you away,' she said quickly. 'I can easily make my own way home.' She suddenly realised that her coat and all her money were still inside the house. Panic gripped her. She would have to go in again.

'Don't be silly, I'll take you home.' Gino was suddenly very Italian. He stared at her as she blinked back her tears. 'You know Farrell's in there,' he said harshly.

Laura took a deep breath. 'Yes.'

'Has he upset you?'

'No! Please, Gino, leave it.' She could not talk about Tom Farrell. If she did she had the feeling she would end up bawling like a baby.

Gino's mouth tightened. 'How can I?' he demanded

huskily. He touched her face very gently. 'I love you, Laura, you know that already. I've noticed the change in you, your carefulness, your worry.'

She stared into his eyes, shaken by his words, and deep sad compassion filled her heart as she looked in to his dark, serious face. I wish I could love you, she thought silently. I now know the anguish of unrequited love and it shouldn't have happened to you, dear Gino, you don't deserve it.

'Gino, I. . . .'

'You don't have to say anything,' he cut in with a swift smile. 'I only told you because you already knew, because I don't want you to be worried or careful and I don't want to spoil or strain the friendship we have. I know you don't love me, you never will, and I have no intention of pushing it. Crazy world, isn't it?' he laughed, without humour. 'But I'll get over it, baby, fall in love with someone else, I don't doubt.' His eyes told her that he did not want pity or any particular kindness, not ever. 'But I want your friendship, it means a lot to me, and I don't want to spoil it just because of these crazy feelings I have.' He paused. 'Do you think we can work something out?'

'I'm sure we can,' Laura whispered, tears in her eyes again. He was so good, so kind, and her heart ached for him. He had never pushed her, never mentioned his feelings before, hiding them completely, accepting the fact that she would never reciprocate his love. Suddenly she smiled. Yes, she and Gino would make it as friends, she knew that for certain.

'We'll always be friends,' she told him, leaning forward to kiss him. His arms came around her and he kissed her back, his mouth warm and gentle on hers, not with passion or hunger but with love and friendship. Laura slid her own arms around his waist, clinging blindly to the comfort he offered, still shaken by his confession, by seeing Tom Farrell again.

A slight noise behind them split them apart and Laura opened dazed eyes to find Tom Farrell in the doorway of the house staring at her. He was obviously leaving. Amanda Delvaux and the man in the dark suit were already on the street walking away, arm in arm, laughing together, but Tom Farrell stood perfectly still, his powerful body silhouetted in the light from within the house, taut with a nameless violence.

Laura stiffened, her hands falling like stones from Gino's waist, forgetting him. They stared at each other. Tom's grey eyes flamed anger, contempt at her, his mouth tight and bitter. She recoiled from the hard violence in him, and lowered her eyes, shivering.

Gino turned slowly, inclining his head. 'Tom.' As he acknowledged the other man's presence, he slipped his arm round Laura's shoulder, bringing her close to him, sensing her fear. Tom Farrell muttered something cool and fairly polite, that Laura did not catch, but he was ignoring Gino completely, his eyes destroying Laura, holding her gaze with their brilliance, their violence.

She turned away, her heart hammering wildly, and when she dared to look up again he was gone, indolent and silent, into the darkness of the night, where Amanda Delvaux no doubt waited for him.

CHAPTER SIX

WEDNESDAY morning came quickly and Laura was unprepared. She felt lethargic and depressed after the unsettling incident at the party.

Gino helped her organise herself and pack. The hands of the clock crept past nine o'clock and Laura began to panic. 'Oh God, Grace will be here in less than an hour!' she moaned, running a distracted hand through her hair.

'Relax!' Gino smiled goodnaturedly, and pushed her into a chair. 'Everything is under control.' He poured out some coffee for her and handed her a cigarette. 'Now sit down for five minutes and we can check you've not forgotten anything.'

She grinned at him, thankful for his help. 'I don't know what I'd do without you,' she told him, sipping her coffee gratefully.

'Neither do I,' he laughed cheerfully. By ten to ten, miraculously, Laura was ready, her two suitcases and a box of provisions standing by the door ready to go.

She switched off the electricity and handed the keys to Gino so that he could keep an eye on the place while she was away. 'You will come and stay for a weekend if you get the chance, won't you?' she said pleadingly. 'Grace and the kids would love you to.'

'Sure.' He was pleased by her invitation. 'I'll telephone you.'

'Which reminds me——' Laura rummaged in her bag for the number Grace had given her, 'there's the number of the cottage. You'll ring?' He nodded, tucking the scrap of paper into the pocket of his jeans.

Then Grace arrived, looking as distracted as Laura had felt an hour before. Laura offered coffee, but Grace refused, explaining that the children were fighting in the car, and the sooner they were on their way the better. 'You can still change your mind you know,' she said, half humorously, half seriously.

'I wouldn't dream of it,' Laura told her firmly. 'I need this break.'

Gino carried her cases down to Grace's car and stowed them in the boot. He kissed Laura's cheek. 'Be happy, and enjoy yourself,' he instructed.

And suddenly they were driving away, Laura in the back with an excited Jan and Christy in the front with his mother, all of them waving to Gino. It was a long tiring journey that took all day and evening. Even frequent leisurely stops at motorway service stations did not help much, and by late afternoon the children were fractious and noisy and Laura and Grace, sharing the driving, were worn out.

Still, Laura reflected as she turned the car off the motorway, it certainly put all her other problems out of her mind. They stopped for dinner at a hotel near the main road. The food was good, the atmosphere relaxing and the children, tired out, were quiet and well behaved. 'We should have flown,' Grace said ruefully as they climbed back in the car.

'Too easy,' Laura replied, switching on the engine. 'Besides, it's not so bad now.'

Grace laughed, glancing over her shoulder at the children, wrapped in blankets and falling asleep. 'Blessed silence!' And so the rest of the journey passed quite pleasantly, Grace reading the map and navigating, both girls smoking and chatting.

The roads became worse and worse, smaller and smaller. It was pitch black, the car headlights being their only guide, but at last, as they bumped down a tiny dirt track, the headlights revealed a long, white-washed cottage. 'This must be it!' Grace exclaimed excitedly, jumping out of the car to check.

It was, and Laura switched off the engine with relief, knowing it was too dark to see how badly she was parked. It would have to wait until the morning. She slid out of the car, stretching her aching muscles, and breathed deeply of the dark night air. It was cold and clean and smelled of trees and flowers and hills, and there was a faint fresh breeze. It was exhilarating, a different world from London, and a tiny thrill of pleasure ran through her.

She followed Grace into the cottage, gazing around the low-ceilinged room. It was beautiful—white walls and low oak beams, tiny, deeply set windows, comfortable-looking chintz-covered chairs and dark wood furniture, with a black iron grate beneath the carved mantelpiece. Grace smiled at her. 'Lovely, isn't it?' Laura agreed, her eyes shining. It was perfect, exactly how a cottage in the country should be. 'I'll go and fetch the kids,' said Grace, heading for the door resignedly.

'I'll bring the cases,' and Laura followed her out.

Half an hour later Jan and Christy were tucked up in bed in a tiny attic room containing bunk beds. Laura had lit a small fire in the grate and Grace had made coffee. 'It was definitely worth the drive,' Laura said contentedly, stretching out her legs towards the glow of the fire.

'Mm, it's got a wonderful atmosphere,' Grace agreed, offering her friend a cigarette.

Coffee finished Laura staggered to her feet, yawning.

'I'm exhausted, shall we leave everything until the morning?' Grace did not need much persuading. Upstairs they found two tiny bedrooms and a bathroom. Laura washed tiredly, then undressed, glancing round the bedroom with pleasure. There was only room for a brass bed, covered in a rose-patterned quilt, a small but beautiful mahogany chest with an oval mirror and brass handles, and a small matching wardrobe. The wooden floorboards were polished and covered by bright, plaited rag rugs. She flung open the window and the night air drifted into the room, gently moving the thin lace curtains. She climbed into the bed. It was soft, so soft, and she sank into it, her tired body relaxing immediately. She was asleep before her head touched the pillows.

She was woken at dawn by the birds outside, and struggled into wakefulness, lying perfectly still, forgetting where she was for a second. Then she remembered, her eyes moving around the room that was bathed in the pinky-gold light of dawn.

She listened to the birds' extraordinarily sweet singing, it touched something inside her, and suddenly she was crying, tears running soft and silently down her face. She did not want to wake alone. She had been dreaming of Tom. They had been walking together in sunlight-dappled woods, absurdly romantic. His arm had been strong and heavy around her shoulders as he had made her laugh, touched his mouth to hers. His grey eyes had been so gentle in that dream, but she vividly remembered the contempt, the violence in them the last time she had seen him. She could not bear it. She turned her wet face into the pillow and incredibly fell asleep again.

She was re-awakened three hours later by Christy, his tongue stuck out in concentration as he tried to carry a cup of coffee without spilling any.

'We've been up for ages,' he told her scornfully. 'And we've had breakfast.'

'Good for you!' Laura smiled, sitting up and taking the coffee from his small hands.

'You should get up too,' he told her, nodding his head for emphasis.

'I will, in a minute,' she replied, unable to stop herself laughing. He was so sweet and sincere and serious, surveying her unwaveringly from beneath his untidy fringe. 'Okay,' he said doubtfully, and bounded out of the room.

Laura sipped her coffee slowly, enjoying it. It was a sunny day, the room bright, cool with the faint scented breeze that wafted through the open window. She got out of bed and stuck her head outside, gasping with pleasure at the beautiful view that met her eyes. A wild untidy garden ran from the house to a glinting fast-running river, only about fifty yards away. On the river bank trees and beyond them, hills, fields and not a building in sight. It certainly was the back of beyond, exactly what she had hoped for. Whoever owned this cottage was very lucky. It had been renovated to include all modern conveniences, so although it was very comfortable, the peace and the slow, sleepy atmosphere had not been destroyed. It was the sort of house Laura would have liked to have as a permanent home. She remembered that she had not asked Grace who it belonged to. She would ask at breakfast.

Showering in the tiny pink-tiled bathroom was a pleasure and she dressed in tight serviceable blue jeans and a blue tee-shirt. The kitchen was empty, a hasty note scrawled by Grace told her that her friend had taken the car and the children to the nearest village in search of bread and fresh milk.

After a quick breakfast of coffee and toast, Laura

unpacked her cases and made her bed, placing the silver casket that Tom had given her on the small chest of drawers. It shone in the sunlight like a precious jewel, somehow seeming at home in the tiny cottage bedroom. She had brought it with her automatically, unable to leave it behind.

She wandered downstairs, where everywhere was tidy, and out into the garden. It was incredibly hot and bright. Insects buzzed past her ear, birds sang, and it was such a pleasure to have grass beneath her feet instead of concrete. She strolled down to the river, the brightness of the water hurting her eyes, and sat down with her back against a tree trunk, lifting her face to the sun. It was so good to do nothing. Her mind, tight and sharp and pained, seemed to relax as she sat in the sun, to slow down a little. Yes, she needed this break. She closed her eyes and let her thoughts drift into nothing, lazily concentrating on the hushed roar of the river.

Suddenly something cold and wet touched her hand as it lay loosely in her lap, and she opened her eyes in wary alarm, laughing as she saw the big black dog. It was enormous, sleek and solid, she did not recognise the breed. She stroked its head gently and it licked her hand. 'Where are you from, boy?' she asked smilingly, and the dog, wagging its tail, pricked up its ears at her voice. Seconds later another dog, identical to the one at her side, bounded through the long grass towards her, followed by a tall young man.

He stopped in front of her. 'Hi. I hope the dogs aren't bothering you.' He had a slow, easy smile.

'Not at all,' she answered, examining him with interest. She guessed he was about twenty, his brown hair hanging to his shoulders, and there was a strong air of self-assurance about him, curious in one so young. He had a strong intelligent face, grey eyes and a firm generous mouth and he wore only faded jeans, his chest bare, firmly muscled yet lean. All in all he was a very attractive boy, Laura decided, as he squatted beside her, pushing his hair back from his face.

'I'm Luke,' he said, staring at her.

'Laura,' she replied.

'Did you arrive last night?' he asked, idly throwing a stick for the dogs.

'Yes, but. . . .'

'My father owns the house you're staying in. Is everything to your satisfaction?'

She smiled at his formality. 'Yes, it's fine. Do you live near?'

He pointed along the river. 'You can't see the house from here, it's just behind those trees.'

Laura suddenly realised that he had no accent. 'You're not Scottish, are you?'

He shook his head, smiling. 'I was brought up in France—my parents are English, though. You have the same colouring as my mother. She looks a little like you, in fact, but only a little. You're more beautiful, much more beautiful.'

There was a sweet sincerity in his casual words and Laura flushed with embarrassment, watching the dogs as they flopped on to their sides in the grass, tongues hanging out. 'Thank you,' she said confusedly. 'You live with your parents, then?' she continued, finding that she was curious about him.

He stretched out beside her, his arms behind his head. There was a careless grace in his movements that drew her eyes, reminding her of. . . . She blocked the thought from her mind in fevered dismay.

'My father's in London at the moment. I'm here alone,' he replied lazily.

Laura realised that she had questioned him enough. She did not want to sound like the Spanish Inquisition. She closed her eyes again. 'It's so hot,' she murmured drowsily.

Luke laughed. 'It won't last. The local people are talking about floods before the end of the month.'

'How pessimistic!' She forced open her eyes and looked at the river. 'How can they tell?'

He shrugged. 'I don't know, but they can.'

'I can't believe it,' she said. 'It's too peaceful.'

'Calm before the storm?' he suggested, and she laughed.

'Maybe.'

She turned to look at him and found that he was watching her, long dark lashes shading his eyes. She looked away.

'Where are you from?' he asked lazily.

'London. And I was glad to get away. I think I'm fed up with living in the city,' she said truthfully.

'It's not so bad,' Luke replied. 'The place doesn't really matter, it's the people.' There was no particular expression in his voice, but she sensed the bitterness in him and the perception. She turned her head again and met his grey eyes. 'And you're running away,' he stated softly, his voice sure.

'Yes, I suppose I am,' she admitted, thinking of Tom with a sharp rush of longing. Why had she admitted it to this young stranger?

She put her hands down on the grass intending to lever herself to her feet, but her fingers encountered a clump of stinging nettles and she was badly stung, all along her hand and fingers up to her wrist. She could not help her small cry of pain, nursing her hand as the small white lumps appeared. Luke was beside her immediately. 'Nettles,' she explained, biting her lower lip. She had never imagined they could be so painful, her whole hand was throbbing, as though it was on fire.

Luke walked away, his eyes on the ground, and returned a moment later with a handful of large dark green leaves. He crouched at her side and gently took her hand. 'Dock leaves,' he said, in answer to her curious glance. 'They'll take away the pain.' He rubbed her swollen skin with the leaves and miraculously they worked, taking the fire from her skin almost immediately.

She gazed at Luke's bent head, at the tanned skin of his shoulders as he worked on her hand. He raised his head, pushing back his hair in what she realised was a characteristic gesture, and as their eyes met, she knew that he was attracted to her.

In panic she turned away, pulling free her hand. 'Thanks, that's much better,' she said quietly. He flashed her that warm easy smile.

'Does it deserve a cup of coffee?'

'Yes, I think it does.' Laura could not help smiling back, and they walked slowly to the cottage together, the two black dogs bounding behind them. There was no sign of Grace or the children. Luke sat down at the kitchen table after ordering the dogs to stay outside and watched her as she ground the coffee beans.

'What will you do while you're here?' he asked casually.

She shrugged. 'As little as possible. I just want to relax.'

'Will you come riding with me tomorrow?'

'I can't ride,' she replied, sitting down at the table while she waited for the percolator.

'I can teach you—you'll enjoy it. You're too pale.'

He was teasing her, and why not? she thought. He was a pleasant companion.

'Yes, all right, I'll come—if Grace doesn't need me,' she agreed.

'Grace?'

'My friend. She's gone to buy some bread.' It sounded so funny that they both laughed. The coffee was ready and they chatted about nothing in particular while they drank it.

Then Luke got to his feet, stretching his brown arms lazily above his head. 'I'll see you tomorrow, mid-afternoon. I'll bring the horses.' He smiled at her and strolled away, whistling for the dogs who followed enthusiastically. Laura watched him go from the doorway of the cottage. She liked him.

Grace returned half an hour later, looking flustered, and shouting at the children. Laura ran out to the car and took the cardboard box containing fresh provisions from her friend's arms. 'You should have woken me, I'd have come with you,' she said apologetically.

'You needed a rest,' Grace replied firmly.

'Well, it's your turn now,' said Laura, just as firmly. 'I'll give the children their lunch and you can have an official child-free afternoon off, okay?' And when Grace opened her mouth to protest, she added, 'Starting right now! Have a rest, go for a walk, anything, but leave the cottage, the children and all the responsibilities to me.' Her tone brooked no argument and Grace smiled. 'Thanks. I think I'll walk down by the river, it's such a wonderful day. Are you sure you. . . ?'

'Away you go. I can cope,' Laura assured her, walking towards the kitchen, the children, obedient for once, trailing behind her. 'See you later!'

She watched from the window as Grace walked

away. We're two miserable women, she thought wryly, trying to pretend that there's nothing wrong. Why do we pretend, I wonder?

She washed the children's hands and gave them baked beans on toast, followed by ice cream for their lunch, and in the relative peace while they ate, stored away the bread and milk Grace had bought in the village.

Jan slept after lunch and Laura helped Christy with a huge jigsaw she found in the box of toys they had brought with them from home. They carried a table into the garden and worked on the bright jigsaw outside in the sun. It was pleasant, soothing to sit in the garden playing and talking with a small intelligent child, and Laura enjoyed herself immensely.

Grace returned before dinner, cheeks flushed from the fresh air, infinitely more cheerful. Laura prepared spaghetti bolognese for dinner and they sat and talked the evening away. And as she climbed into bed some hours later she reflected on what a good day it had been.

The next afternoon, as promised, Luke arrived leading two horses. Laura and Grace were sitting by the river after a picnic lunch, Jan and Christy playing ball nearby. Christy's squeal of delight as he spotted the horses turned both girl's heads.

Laura, shading her eyes with her hand watched Luke's approach with a smile. 'Hi,' he greeted her cheerfully. 'Ready for your first lesson?'

'I suppose so,' she replied, looking doubtfully at the horses. They seemed enormous! 'I'm beginning to have second thoughts, though.'

'Too late.' His eyes mocked her gently.

She sighed and got to her feet. 'Luke, I'd like to introduce you to Grace, Jan and Christy. Grace, children, this is Luke.'

Grace held out her hand. 'Hello, Luke,' she grinned at him. 'This I've got to see—have you actually got Laura to *agree* to get on a horse?'

Luke laughed. 'I surely have. You'll be able to see it with your own eyes.'

'Can I have a go too?' Christy demanded, staring up at Luke with a kind of awed respect.

'When Laura's had her go,' Luke promised, his eyes on Laura, warm and amused.

'Great!' Christy practically jumped up and down with excitement.

'Me too! Me too!' Jan tugged at Luke's hand, her eyes filling with quick tears, fearing she would be left out.

'Yes, you too,' Luke assured her, gently squeezing her tiny hand. His eyes found Laura's again. 'Okay, Laura, time to get it over with.'

She frowned at him, mock-angry. 'Thanks very much!'

They walked over to the horses, who ignored them as they approached, heads down munching at the long grass. 'This one is yours,' Luke told her, indicating an *enormous* brown beast. 'Her name is Amber and she's very placid and sweet-tempered.'

'And big!' Laura added apprehensively. Luke shook his head, silent with laughter. 'Put your left foot into the stirrup and lift yourself on to her back.' She did as he said, and easily and suddenly she was on the horse, looking down at him with a triumphant smile. 'See, that wasn't so difficult.'

'No,' she had to agree, still not feeling very confident even so. Luke passed her the reins and swung himself up on to the other horse, sitting confidently, obviously no stranger to riding.

In the hour that followed Laura learned a great

deal, gradually gaining confidence until she was actually enjoying herself. There was only one moment of panic, when Amber picked up speed, breaking into a canter as she followed Luke's horse. Laura shouted, paralysed with fear, finding that she couldn't control the horse, and Luke slowed, calmly telling her what to do, and the horror passed as the horse finally obeyed her.

They ended up about a mile from the cottage. Laura was completely lost, but Luke led the way down to the river, the horses splashing in the shallow water, walking side by side beneath the trees towards the cottage. Sunlight shivered through the overhead branches, cool and bright, the water glinting, spraying from the horses' hooves, noisy, cold and refreshing. Laura felt very happy. She smiled at Luke beside her, the sun in her golden hair giving her face a fragile ethereal beauty.

'It's lovely. Thanks for teaching me.'

He pushed back his long hair. 'I wanted to,' he replied seriously. The dappled light gleamed on his tanned shoulders, bared by the sleeveless vest he wore, on his wild dark hair. He looks like a strong young god, Laura thought fancifully, a warrior riding into battle.

'Crazy, isn't it, that in twenty-three years I've never been on a horse before,' she remarked lazily.

'You've always lived in the city?'

'Yes, how about you?'

'I've lived in many places, but I guess Nice is the place where I've spent most of my life.'

'Do you work?' Again Laura felt a rising curiosity about him. Instinct told her that he was no ordinary, run-of-the-mill young man, and he intrigued her.

'No, I'm still deciding whether or not I want to go

to university,' he replied with a faint grimace.

'How old are you?' The question was out before she realised how nosey it sounded. However, Luke did not seem to take offence.

'Nineteen—just,' he smiled.

She was surprised. For some reason she had imagined he was older, he certainly seemed older. 'I'm sorry,' she apologised quickly. 'You must think I'm very nosey.'

'Not at all, I'm flattered by your interest.' His eyes were wicked with amusement as he spoke.

They rounded a bend in the river and the cottage came in sight. Christy and Jan spotted the horses immediately and ran towards them. But Laura's eyes were drawn to Grace and the tall, familiar figure of the man talking by her side. As they drew nearer she recognised him and the colour drained from her face, her heartbeat stopping altogether for one desperate second. It was Tom Farrell, the last person in the world she had expected to see. I must be dreaming, she thought wildly, it can't be him, it just can't be!

But Luke had also recognised the man who sat so indolently at Grace's side. 'Tom's here,' he remarked with a certain calm pleasure.

Still very dazed, Laura turned to him. 'What?' she echoed confusedly.

'Tom,' he repeated patiently. 'My father.'

CHAPTER SEVEN

IF she had been shocked at seeing Tom Farrell, her amazement deepened a thousandfold at Luke's calm revelation. He was *Tom's son*. She repeated the words in her head. Tom's son. It seemed beyond belief. It *must* be a dream, she told herself again and again. One of those dark and crazy upside-down dreams in which people and places interlock in weird, unbelievable patterns.

But as she watched Tom move with slow easy grace to his feet, as the horses stopped, she was forced to accept the fact that it was no dream, he was actually here in Scotland, and amazingly, impossibly, Luke was his son.

She felt Tom's eyes moving over her, dark and unfathomable, and lowered her head, letting the shining curtain of her hair swing protectively over her flushed cheeks. Luke slid from his horse, telling her how to dismount, catching her as she almost fell. For a second she felt the young strength of his arms around her, his hands at her waist as he steadied her. Their eyes met, his very serious, the pupils dilated. She smiled her thanks at him, selfconscious, still wide-eyed with shock and he released her with obvious reluctance.

Looking up, she caught Tom's gaze as he watched her with Luke. His grey eyes held a cold blank anger, his mouth a hard straight line, and suddenly a strange violent tension was buzzing between them.

Luke broke the spell, smiling at the man, who incredibly was his father. 'I'm glad you've come,' he said quietly. And knowing that she was safe from that destroying blank gaze, Laura watched them from beneath her lashes as they greeted each other and saw the warm bond of love and mutual friendship and respect between them.

Tom's eyes were gentle, smiling as he talked to Luke. Once she had known that gentleness and had thrown it back in his face. A sad haunting pain gripped her heart, as the knowledge of how much she loved him hit her. It seemed impossible yet was desperately true. In the short time since she had last seen him she had missed him so badly. Her eyes flicked over him hungrily, as he stood with his hands resting lightly on his hips, unaware of her scrutiny. The sunlight gleamed on his vital dark hair, along the polished hardness of jaw and cheekbone, giving his skin the glow of oiled wood. He wore faded jeans that clung to the lean strength of his hips and a white collarless shirt. She watched every tiny movement he made with aching intensity, aware of every restless shifting of his long powerful legs, every impatient hand thrust through the darkness of his hair, every graceful lift of his wide shoulders. She also watched Luke and recognised the resemblance between them. It was amazing that she had not seen it before. Perhaps subconsciously she had, and that was what had drawn her to Luke. The self-assurance, the smooth grace, the grey eyes—Tom's were more cynical, more world-weary, but the colour was exactly the same.

Suddenly she remembered something Luke had said the day they had met. 'You have the same colouring as my mother. She looks a little like you, in fact.' Bitterness almost choked her. Was that why Tom had pursued her, because she resembled his wife? The thought filled her with nameless, jealous anger and she turned away abruptly, not wanting to look at him any more, noticing how heavy the sky had become. The sun was still hot and bright, but it now shone with a sullen threat, the sky somehow menacing.

Perspiration trickled down her spine, sticking her shirt uncomfortably to her body, cold moisture suddenly beading her forehead. She had the most dreadful feeling of foreboding. She noticed also that Grace was staring at her, eyes worried, pleading, and flashed her what she hoped was a reassuring smile. Then another thought struck her. Tom Farrell owned the cottage they were staying in. Grace must have known all along and not bothered to tell her.

She felt trapped and the feeling of foreboding intensified inside her. Had Grace known that Tom was coming? Paranoia, she told herself with a faintly bitter smile. They'll be locking you up if you carry on like this!

She gazed at the river, hearing Grace laughing with Tom and Luke. She heard her own name mentioned and knew that she would have to acknowledge Tom's presence sooner or later. So with a great effort of will, she turned back to the three people who stood on the river bank, and raised apprehensive eyes.

'Hello, Laura,' Tom said coolly. 'Enjoying your holiday?'

She bristled at the cold cynicism in his voice. I was until you arrived, she wanted to say, but the fact that Grace and Luke were listening prevented her. 'Hello, Mr Farrell,' she managed just as coolly as he, her violet eyes wide and scornful. 'Thank you, I'm enjoying myself immensely.' Her glance slid to Luke and she smiled at him, fully aware that Tom's eyes were frozen coldly on that action.

'You two know each other?' Luke enquired with surprise.

Before Tom said anything Laura answered quickly, 'I did some work for your father recently.' Even to her own ears the words sounded disinterested, dismissive, a clear indication to anybody listening of what she thought of Tom Farrell. She heard the faint hiss of Tom's indrawn breath and waited, bowed with inevitability, for him to destroy her with cold words. He could embarrass her completely with one or two well chosen sentences, she was as aware of that as he was. But incredibly he remained silent and Luke seemed satisfied with her explanation. Tension once again filled the air around them and Laura felt an overpowering need to get away.

She turned to Grace. 'I'm very hot, I think I'll go inside for a while.' Ignoring Tom completely, she turned her eyes in Luke's direction. 'Thanks again for the riding lesson. Excuse me. . . .'

She began to walk up the garden, and Luke followed her. 'I'll be glad to give you another lesson,' he said quickly, earnestly.

'I'd like that,' she answered, trying not to sound too noncommittal because she knew that if she was careless, she would hurt him. But he seemed to get the message.

'I'll see you soon, then.'

She stopped and smiled at him. 'Yes. And, Luke . . . I'm sorry . . . it's just that I feel very tired.'

It was weak and they both knew it. 'You don't like Tom, do you?' he questioned directly, his eyes telling her that he could not understand it.

'Why should you think that?' she parried, as lightly as she could. She could feel Tom's eyes on her as surely as though he was physically touching her.

Luke shrugged. She had not fooled him for a second. 'Okay, you don't want to talk about it.'

'No, I don't.' She paused, longing for escape. 'I'll see you in a day or two.' He nodded, giving in, and she walked back to the house.

Determined not to look out of the window even though she longed to, Laura flung herself into a chair and lit a cigarette. She hoped she hadn't been rude to Luke, after all she could hardly blame him for being Tom's son. She blew out a number of perfect smoke rings and watched them drifting up into the air, breaking up slowly. Why had Tom come here, and why should she suppose it had anything to do with her? Logically, she realised, his son was here in Scotland, so there was absolutely no reason why he should not be here. Monumental vanity, she thought wearily, and the fact that she loved him so much. It was all a dreadful coincidence, him arriving like this. She might not even see him again. After the things she had said to him she could hardly expect him to seek out her company.

Her thoughts were interrupted by Grace entering the room. She still looked worried. 'Laura. . . .'

'Why didn't you tell me Tom Farrell owns this cottage?' Laura cut in without preamble.

Grace sat down. 'I should have done, I know,' she admitted slowly.

'So why didn't you? You must have known——?' Laura broke off and lit another cigarette, her hands tense and nervous.

'I thought you wouldn't come if I told you,' Grace said quietly.

'I probably wouldn't have,' Laura replied tiredly.

'There was no deceit involved,' said Grace, leaning forward earnestly. 'Honestly. I knew he owned the cottage, of course, but I didn't think it mattered—well, maybe I did and that's why I didn't tell you, because I knew you two weren't getting on very well.' She paused at Laura's short humourless laugh. 'I needed to get out of London and I needed your help. I was as surprised as you when Tom turned up this afternoon. I'm sorry.'

Laura took one look at Grace's face and felt thoroughly ashamed of herself. 'Oh, Grace, I'm sorry, I know I'm blowing it up out of all proportion. So he owns this cottage, so what? You were right, it doesn't matter. It's my own stupid fault for falling in love with him.'

Grace almost gasped with surprise. 'You love him?'

'Well and truly.'

'But isn't there any chance that——?'

'No,' Laura cut in quickly and flatly. 'Not a single chance.'

Grace stared at her. 'The way he was looking at you this afternoon—I wouldn't say he was indifferent, by any means.'

'I can assure you it's not love—dislike maybe, but not love.' Laura could not hide her misery.

She told Grace very briefly what had happened between Tom and herself, glossing over the worst scenes, and when she had finished Grace asked gently, 'Do you want to go back to London?'

Laura thought about it, but her pride came to the rescue. Why should she run away? She certainly couldn't imagine Tom Farrell having any sleepless nights over her and the fact that she was staying in his cottage. She would not let Grace down. 'No,' she said decisively, 'I want to stay.'

'Are you sure?' Her friend's face told her that she must only stay if she wanted to for herself.

'Yes, there's no point in running away, I can't get him out of my mind anyway.' A thought intruded. 'Did you know about Luke?'

To her relief Grace shook her head. 'Incredible, isn't it? I had no idea Tom had a son—mind you, my not knowing doesn't surprise me. I don't suppose many people know, Tom's a very private person. When I saw them together, though, I wondered why I hadn't realised before—those grey eyes—a dead giveaway.'

Laura nodded in agreement. Whenever she thought about Luke being Tom Farrell's son she felt dazed, absolutely astounded.

She got to her feet as Christy and Jan pounded into the room. 'I'll make some tea,' she said, wanting to do something ordinary and reassuring, to take her mind off Tom and Luke, for a while at least. That was the best she could hope for.

Four hours later the sun had gone completely, the sky was a strange ominous green. Laura leaned out of her bedroom window, amazed at the silence; even the birds had stopped singing. The air was hot and heavy. It was almost frightening the sense of stillness, of waiting. Grace had retired to bed with a migraine after dinner and the children had been asleep for over an hour. Laura felt tired, drained even, but she was terribly restless, her mood aggravated by the threatening weather.

Sighing, she shut the bedroom window and wandered downstairs into the garden. It was still and hot and she did not need a jacket. She walked through the trees by the river, kicking her feet in the dry grass as the sky became darker and darker, faint rumblings issuing from its far corners. A storm, she thought with satisfaction and a certain amount of anticipation. It would clear the air and perhaps her mind as well. She began to walk faster along the river bank in an effort to burn off the restless energy that filled her. She was going nowhere in particular, but walking so fast gave her a sense of purpose, of direction, however illusory.

The sky was a dark grey-green now, almost night and she stumbled once or twice in the long grass, not noticing the dark figure of a man blocking her path some yards ahead until she was right in front of him. She could not see his face in the darkness, he was surrounded in shadow, and a strange panic gripped her. Why had she been walking alone at night—it was utterly stupid! She veered away at right angles to him, wondering how far she was from the cottage, wondering if she could run properly in the sandals she was wearing. Her heart was beating very fast, her eyes wide with fear. He was so silent.

Then he moved, lightning-fast, out of the shadows, directly into her path, and softly spoke her name. It was Tom Farrell, and her relief was matched by her anger with him for frightening her so.

'You!' she gasped, her breath coming sharply. 'What on earth do you think you're doing, lurking in the trees and nearly giving me a heart attack!' She glared up into his lean face, her violet eyes huge and defiant.

He stared down at her. 'What on earth do you think you're doing, walking alone on a night like this?' he enquired coldly, mocking her by repeating what she had said.

Her teeth clenched together with sheer frustration. 'Mind your own damned business,' she muttered furiously. 'Just leave me alone.'

She swung away from him intending to run, but he reached for her, his long fingers curling around her arm, cool and very tight, easily detaining her. 'Why so angry, I wonder?' he murmured softly, the hard line of his mouth ironic, as though he could read her inner turmoil, as though he knew of her love for him.

The touch of his fingers on her bare arm, even though he was touching her in anger, sent a wave of languorous weakness through her body, and she hated herself for that response to him. He was playing games with her and she was more than ready to fall into his arms. Her gentle mouth tightened into a fierce straight line and her eyes flashed impotent fury at him. She tried to shake her arm free, without success.

'Perhaps I don't like being pawed by a married man!' she almost spat at him. His fingers tightened bruisingly on her arm but his face remained impassive.

'Of course, I'd forgotten. Teenage boys are more to your taste,' he drawled hatefully.

Laura gasped as the insult hit home. Acting on pure instinct, she swung her free hand up to hit him, but he caught her wrist before it was even halfway to his face, twisting both her arms behind her back, holding both in one of his hands so that her body was arched towards him. He clucked his tongue maddeningly.

'I've warned you about that before.' He almost smiled. 'So fragile and so beautiful, yet so violent. That temper of yours is going to get you into trouble one of these fine days.'

Laura stared at him, speechless and so angry that she felt she might burst. Electricity crackled between them as their eyes fought a silent battle, and hers dropped first under that steady, unfathomable grey gaze.

Her body was almost touching his and she twisted impotently, knowing the immense strength of his arms, the weakening nearness of him. Then suddenly she stopped fighting; it was, after all, very pointless. 'I think it already has,' she said quietly, a faint smile playing at the corners of her mouth. She could feel the hysteria bubbling up in the light of the ridiculous situation she found herself in.

Whatever Tom had expected her to say it was clearly not that, and he stared down at her, his eyes softening at her self-deprecating smile.

'If I let you go will you promise not to attack me again?' he asked teasingly, his quick smile warm and very charming.

'I can't promise anything,' she replied firmly, her breath catching as she looked up at him.

Tom raised one dark eyebrow. 'I guess I'll just have to take my chances, then.' He released her arms, watching as she rubbed her sore wrists. 'Did I hurt you?' There was a strange husky note in his voice as he asked.

'Are you worried?' she parried dryly.

'It wasn't my intention, but God knows you can use your tongue like poison.' His mouth twisted wryly.

'You're not too bad in that department yourself,' she retorted, slanting him a glance from beneath her long lashes. The moment of terrible tension between them had passed and she was very relieved.

Tom laughed, his strong teeth glinting in the dim light. 'How about a truce?'

She considered that suggestion in silence. 'I suppose we could try,' she answered doubtfully.

He shook his head, laughing. 'Such enthusiasm— you really are an expert at bolstering a man's ego!'

Laura laughed too. Tom Farrell needed nobody to bolster his ego. 'In my experience that's the last thing most men need. An over-inflated ego is the worst complaint of the male sex,' she said tartly.

'Your experience?' he queried in a soft drawl. 'Now that sounds like an interesting topic of conversation.'

Laura flushed. 'You'll be lucky!'

His smile was slow and very confident. 'I know I will.' She tutted loudly and turned away. He really was impossible!

The sky was still growling like a hungry lion and the wind was rising now, whipping Laura's pale hair around her face, howling sadly through the trees. She felt very alive, attuned to the elements and desperately aware of the powerfully attractive man behind her. She turned back to him.

'Will it rain?'

'It will rain like hell, you'd better get back.'

She shook her head. She did not want to go back to the cottage, she wanted to stay with him. Even realising how dangerous an impulse it was, she could not fight it. 'I want to walk,' she said sweetly.

'Walk with me, then,' he suggested softly, slipping an arm casually around her shoulders.

'Yes.' Her voice was merely above a whisper, his touch, casual as it was, disturbed her so.

They walked together over the bone-dry grass through the whispering trees. Tom seemed to have the ability to see in the dark, guiding her over the uneven ground and supporting her when she almost fell. It was incredible, Laura thought, that they should be walking together almost at peace, his arm protectively coiled around her shoulders while the elements prepared themselves for a furious battle that seemed as though it might tear the world around them apart. Déjà vu, she thought, remembering her dream.

Tom looked down at her suddenly. 'By the way, I didn't get the chance to thank you for your illustration. I'm sure you know that it's perfect—sensitive perceptive, brilliantly executed. You're very talented, little one, and it'll be an honour to publish it with the play.'

She felt a sweet rush of pleasure at his complimentary words, together with a stab of envy as he
reminded her of Amanda Delvaux, standing in the
doorway of his house, clad only in thin blue silk.

'Thank you,' she murmured huskily, her face flushed
with hectic colour, and on impulse added. 'You can
keep the original if you like—a present in return for
the silver casket.' He was silent, and embarrassment
overcame her. 'You don't have to, of course . . . I don't
. . . that is, I didn't. . . .'

'I know, and thank you, I'd love to keep it,' Tom
said gently, smiling down at her his arm around her
shoulders tightening for a second. They walked on and
despite herself Laura could not get Amanda Delvaux
out of her mind. Was she with Tom in Scotland?

'How long will you stay?' she asked, and as soon as
she had, wished she hadn't.

'Anxious to be rid of me?' His tone was faintly sar-
donic. She did not answer. It was better not to know
how long he'd be here. Tom pinned her with merciless
grey eyes. 'You get on well with Luke?' It was more a
statement of fact than a question, but she could read
no expression in his voice. For some reason she was
instantly on the defensive.

'Why do you want to know?' she demanded defiantly.

'I don't think I do.' There was a definite boredom
in his voice now. 'I merely want to tell you to let him
alone.'

'Meaning?' Her temper was rising at his interfering
arrogance, their truce forgotten as tension, incan-
descent and mercurial, flared between them again.
Every word was double-edged, razor-sharp.

'Meaning that you seem to make a habit of leading
young men on. You've got a chain round Premoli's

neck—isn't that enough without adding Luke to your conquests?' His voice was totally flat, uninterested and very insulting.

Laura gasped. 'How dare you!' she whispered, incensed.

'I dare because my son is already infatuated with you and I don't want him hurt. Got it?'

'A bit late, isn't it?' she retorted, stung into spitefulness.

'And what the hell is that supposed to mean?'

They had stopped walking, standing face to face as they fought. Tom's eyes glittered dangerously, but Laura ignored the warning in them, reckless with anger and pain. 'Your show of concern. I would have thought it was a bit late in the day for you to be coming over all paternal.' The harsh, tightly-angry lines of his face warned her once more, to stop, but she *hated* him at that moment and wanted to hurt him as he had hurt her. 'Tom Farrell, womaniser—quite notorious, aren't you? Your wife tucked away in France, your son in Scotland, while you gallivant around the world. If you expect me to abide by your ridiculous, hypocritical rules you've got another think coming! I happen to like Luke—even though he's your son—and God knows that must be quite a handicap for him. If I want to see him and he wants to see me, we're both over the age of consent and there's absolutely *nothing* you can do about it!'

There was a moment's electric silence and Laura knew that she had gone too far—much too far. She regretted her outburst already. A second later she was dragged hard against his body, his hand ungentle beneath her chin, forcing up her face to his.

'Nothing?' he queried, his voice dangerously soft. 'Are you sure, you little bitch?' He lowered his dark head slowly his grey eyes burning, mesmerising her. She moaned softly as his mouth touched hers, his kiss savage, merciless as he purged his anger against the softness of her lips. She could feel the hard seducing warmth of his body against hers, the clean male scent of his skin filled her nostrils and the strength of his arms made her weak, but she could not respond to the deliberate punishment of his kiss, it was too cruel, and when he finally raised his head she fully expected to see her blood on his mouth, but amazingly there was none. She stared up into the mysterious shadows of his face with wide, hurt eyes. She could feel his hands flat against her spine, possessive in their touch.

He made no move to release her, his gaze holding hers, his anger gone as hers had. 'I can make you forget everything, everybody but me,' he murmured with certainty. 'That's how I'll keep you away from Luke.'

'No. . . .'

'Yes.' He touched his mouth gently to her forehead and a long sweet tremor ran through her.

'Tom, don't . . . please. . . .' He did not heed her pleading. Don't hurt me, she was crying silently, I love you.

'I won't hurt Luke,' she whispered against his smooth hard cheek, giving in.

'I know.' He closed her eyes with his mouth, trailing gentle kisses over her eyelids. 'I know.'

'Then why are you doing this?' she murmured breathlessly, kissing his face. 'Jealousy?'

His voice was hard and low, openly mocking. 'I want you, Laura.'

She shook her head, bewildered. Never in a million years would she believe that he was jealous of his own son. Her hands crept up to his wide, powerful shoulders. She was totally unable to fight her love for him, her need to touch him.

He was still kissing her face, his mouth warm, firm and gentle and she was lost, sweetly and utterly lost. Beneath the silken material of his shirt she could feel the smooth warmth of his skin, the muscles tense, unyielding, and when his mouth finally touched hers she began to tremble violently, her body dissolving in a fierce weak heat. Tom drew her closer, one hand sliding up the curved length of her spine to stroke through her hair, as his mouth explored hers, deeply and hungrily. Laura clung to him, returning his kiss, desperately opening her lips wide to his passionate exploration, as the dark clouds raced low over their heads.

He slowly unfastened the buttons on her thin blouse, exposing her rounded breasts to the sweet touch of his hands. His lips were at her throat, teasing the sensitive skin, his breath coming raggedly, his heart thundering beneath her tense hands.

Then he lifted his dark head slowly, his eyes glittering hungrily on her body, his hands cupping her naked breasts. Laura looked down at those hands, touching her so possessively, so hungrily, staring at the strong tanned fingers, so dark and powerful against her white skin. And she looked into his grey eyes, seeing desire flaring rawly, demanding her response and something else, a fierce tenderness that shook her to her very soul.

'I want you too.' She heard her voice whispering the words, almost lost as his mouth found hers again. He kissed her deeply yet briefly, then held her very tightly against his chest. She did not remember pulling open his shirt, but she must have done because she could feel the rough warmth of his body hair against her aching breasts. They fitted together perfectly, as though specially created for each other.

Tom buried his face in the softness of her hair and murmured her name. It was so slow and unhurried, and unbearably pleasurable, as desire flamed almost out of control. Just to hold each other this way built up a tense desperate need between them. Laura lifted her face from the bare skin of his shoulder and stared into the dark gentle depths of his eyes. Time seemed to stand still. She felt as though she was on the edge of a warm dark precipice, and she was going to jump, lose herself in the darkness that was pleasure and fulfilment.

His taut face descended towards her again, nearer and nearer. As their mouths touched a jagged fork of lightning ripped apart the sky above them, illuminating the harsh planes of his face, the soft lines of hers. It was frightening, and symbolic, their mouths moving hungrily against each other as the sky burst into flames. Seconds later came the thunder, rolling deafeningly in the wake of the blinding light. It was the loudest thunder that Laura had ever heard and she jumped violently, her childhood fear of storms coming back to her. Tom's arms tightened around her, his mouth leaving hers as he sensed her fear, his hand stroking her hair again, soothing her.

And finally came the rain, soft and warm and heavy, soaking them in a moment, plastering their hair to their heads, their clothes to their bodies. They laughed together, arms wrapped round each other. Tom kissed her fiercely, his lips cool and wet.

'I want you,' he murmured against her mouth.

'I want you here and now, in the middle of this storm. I want to make love to you in the wet grass, in the rain, under this incredible sky.' He lifted his head and smiled wryly at her. 'But we'd probably get killed!'

Even as he spoke a branch crashed behind them, shaking the ground beneath their feet, reinforcing his words.

Still weak with desire, Laura smiled too. 'And we're too young to die!'

'I don't think I'd give a damn if you were mine,' he replied half-seriously, kissing her forehead and pulling her blouse around her wet body, fastening it quickly.

'That's the nicest thing you've ever said to me,' she laughed breathlessly.

The dark brows lifted in amusement. 'Stick with me honey, I may do even better!'

He took her hand and keeping well away from the trees they began to walk back. Laura was soaked to the skin, her feet squelching uncomfortably in the mud that had once been the river path, but she lifted her face to the pelting rain and smiled, feeling happier than she had done for weeks. Tom walked beside her, indolent and silent, his open shirt flapping in the wind, his powerful body gleaming with rain, as uncaring of the weather as she was. They did not talk, it would have been virtually impossible, the storm was so loud, but there was a strong bond of peace and contentment between them and all too soon they reached the cottage.

'Would you like some coffee?' Laura asked, loath to let him go. 'We could get dry by the fire.'

He nodded, standing back to let her enter first. The lights were on, but the lounge was empty. Laura found two huge towels, passing one to Tom while she rubbed some of the rain out of her hair. That done, she switched on the percolator in the kitchen and wandered back into the lounge. He was standing in front of the fire absently rubbing the dark hair on his chest with the towel she had given him. He smiled at her as she entered the room and she smiled back, staring, caught in the web of his magnificent virility.

She started to say something, but was cut short by Grace shouting from the bedroom above. 'Laura, is that you?'

'Yes,' Laura called back. 'How are you feeling?'

'Rotten.' The one word was very eloquent. 'There's a phone message for you. Gino rang while you were out. Said he's missing you like hell and could you ring him back—something about the flat, I think.' There was a pause, then, 'Oh yes, and he's thinking of coming up for a weekend——'

'Thanks, I'll ring him,' Laura shouted, before Grace could say anything else. 'Do you want some coffee? I'm making some now.'

'No, I'll see you in the morning.'

Laura felt the colour pouring into her face and from the corner of her eye she could see Tom stiffening, his face closing. Open hostility suddenly filled the small room. He obviously thought the worst about Gino and herself, she realised wearily. What an opinion he must have of her! Gino, Luke, and only half an hour before she had been responding with wild abandon to his lovemaking. She opened her mouth to explain but never got the chance.

Tom moved towards the door silent, fast and furious. 'Forget the coffee,' he said expressionlessly, his grey eyes cold as they skimmed over her wet body.

She glared at him, suddenly angry, hating him for jumping to conclusions. 'I don't know what you think. . . .'

'Forget it,' he repeated harshly, and stepped out into the howling darkness of the storm slamming the door violently behind him. He had walked out on her again.

CHAPTER EIGHT

LAURA stared at the closed door for ages after he had gone, her whole body aching with frustration and sheer injustice. She knew what he thought, of course. He thought she had the morals of an alley-cat and he was probably angry with himself because he had shown her how he desired her. But what really angered her was the unfairness of it all. Presumably it did not matter that Tom was having an affair with Amanda Delvaux, he still considered himself free enough to make love to Laura. Damn him! Why did she have to love him?

When she got up late the next morning it was still raining hard. Surprisingly she felt no ill-effects from her walk in the rain. No physical ill-effects anyway. The remembered touch of Tom's mouth, his hands on her bare skin, his murmured words of desire hung in her mind like rainbows, taunting her, disturbing her.

After a breakfast of coffee and a cigarette, she telephoned Gino. The number rang for ages and she was on the point of hanging up when he sleepily answered. He was very pleased to hear from her, she could hear the pleasure in his voice as he asked, 'How is it up there in the wilds?'

'Raining,' she replied on a faint sigh.

'It's sunny here,' he told her exultantly, then told her all the news from London and she listened with half-hearted interest. 'I wanted to ask you a favour,' he said eventually.

'Ask away.' She closed her eyes and made a deter-

mined effort to banish the terrible depression that held
her in its grip.

'I have some friends coming over from Italy tomorrow. I won't be able to put them all up in here and I
was wondering. . . .'

'If you could use my spare bedrooms? Of course you
can—I owe you a favour, so help yourself,' she said,
staring bleakly at the rain pelting against the window.

'Sure?'

'I've told you, help yourself,' she repeated firmly,
glad to be able to repay him for all he had done for her.

'They'll only be staying until the end of the week,'
he assured her.

'Fine. You've got the key—don't worry.' She
listened to her own voice. She sounded like an old
woman. A grim humourless smile pulled up the corners
of her mouth. Today she felt like an old woman.

'Grace mentioned something about you coming up
for the weekend,' she remembered.

'Yes, next weekend if that suits you.' Gino sounded
so hopeful.

'I'll be glad to see you,' she said, trying to sound
enthusiastic.

She put down the phone five minutes later and
walked over to the window. Such rain! It seemed end-
less. She pushed open one of the small windows and
breathed in the cool damp air. She could hear the faint
roar of the river at the end of the garden, louder than
yesterday, and there was a haze of fine mist around the
treetops. Everything was grey and it matched her mood
completely.

That strange empty restlessness was on her again, so
she pulled on her boots and a coat with a waterproof
hood and stepped out of the front door, colliding with
Luke as she did so.

'Hello.' She did not smile, but her violet eyes were friendly.

'Hi. Walking?' His long hair was soaking his head uncovered.

'Yes, I'm too restless to stay indoors.'

'Mind if I walk with you?' he asked casually, but his eyes were careful as though her answer meant a lot to him.

As they walked through the garden she said, 'Do you know where the nearest shops are?'

Luke nodded. 'It's quite a walk, though. I could drive you there.'

'You have a car?' She peered at him from beneath her hood.

'Tom has a Land Rover, I use that.'

At the mention of Tom's name something froze behind Laura's eyes. 'I . . . I don't want to put you to any trouble. . . .' she began doubtfully, wondering how to turn down his offer.

'It's no trouble, I'd like to. We could have lunch at the pub in the village.'

'Luke——'

'Say yes.' He stared at her with young serious eyes, and Laura shrugged her slim shoulders resignedly. She did not have the mental resources to fight him today. 'Okay, yes.'

Luke smiled and led the way through the trees. Puzzled, she asked, 'Where is this Land Rover?'

'At the house,' he replied unconcernedly.

She stopped dead in her tracks, her face worried. She did not want to see Tom. She could not face him.

'What's the matter?' Luke turned and looked back at her. She was silent. What could she say? 'I'm in love with your father but he despises me and I don't think I could take any of his coldness, his contempt, not today, so I'm sorry, Luke, but I just can't risk bumping into him.' She could imagine Luke's reaction to that.

'Nothing ... I—well, it's just. ...' she stammered, lost for words.

Luke's grey eyes sharpened on her face. 'Tom?' he queried, too perceptively.

Laura's cheeks burned with colour and she turned away. Surely he couldn't know. 'No,' she insisted quickly.

Luke wanted to believe her, his relief was obvious. 'What then?'

There was nothing she could say, no way out of it. If she did bump into Tom she would just have to cope with the situation as best she could. Frigid politeness, perhaps? She had no choice, so she quickly caught up with Luke.

'I'm sorry, my mind is a bit hazy today. I thought I'd forgotten something.' His eyes probed her face disbelievingly, but he said nothing.

They had been walking for about twenty minutes when a house came into view through the trees, a long low cottage, about twice as big as the one Laura and Grace were staying in. Ivy climbed its walls and the roof, though in good repair, was crooked, giving it a beautiful old charm. Two cars were parked outside, one Tom's long black sports car and the other a new-looking Land Rover. Laura felt her heart beating very fast. Please don't let him be here, she prayed silently, her fear coupled with a fierce aching longing for him that angered her.

'Would you like a drink before we set off?' Luke asked, still staring.

Hearing his question with a stab of panic, Laura

carefully schooled her features into what she hoped was a calm mask. 'No, thank you, I've only just had breakfast,' she replied, her eyes cloudy.

'Okay. Hop in.' He pulled open the passenger door of the Land Rover and she climbed in, glancing distractedly at the front door of the house, expecting to see Tom appearing at any moment. But there was no sign of him as the engine roared into life and they sped off down the muddy track towards the road. Laura let her breath out on a silent sigh of relief, her heart gradually slowing as they turned on to the main road.

As Luke had said, the nearest village was quite a distance away and very tiny—a small square, rows of cottages, half a dozen shops and a public house. It was very quiet and Laura could almost feel herself being watched from behind lace-curtained windows as she walked along with Luke at her side. She bought bread and some fresh milk, some sweets for Christy and Jan, a bottle of shampoo and some tissues with no interest whatsoever, her brain and body working mechanically. The shop assistants, mostly middle-aged women, stared at them curiously, although they were all shyly friendly and polite, and Laura emerged into the rain smiling.

'I feel like a foreigner,' she laughed.

Luke took the bulging plastic carrier bag from her hands. 'You are a foreigner,' he teased, gently wiping a raindrop from her nose.

They walked back to the Land Rover and deposited the shopping inside. It was almost one o'clock and they mutually decided that it was time for lunch. Not having eaten any breakfast, Laura found herself ravenous as they entered the tiny old pub. Sitting by the log fire, sipping drinks as they waited for their food, She glanced round with interest, liking the low-beamed ceiling and stone walls. The whole place seemed to gleam with old shiny wood and polished brass. It was original, a far cry from the plastic copies of pubs she knew in London.

'How long have you known Tom?' Luke asked suddenly, striving to be casual.

'Not long,' she replied, just as casually, aware that this conversation could lead her on to very dangerous ground.

'Weeks? Months? Years?' Luke persisted.

'Weeks. As I say, not long at all.' She hoped he would attribute the rush of colour in her face to the heat of the fire.

'Why don't you like him?' Luke seemed unstoppable. She had the feeling he had been brooding about her and Tom.

'I do like him,' she protested vaguely, wanting to laugh. What an understatement! 'Sometimes we don't get on very well, that's all.'

Luke shook his head. 'He's a remarkable man.'

Laura was touched by the love and pride and respect in his eyes. 'Yes,' she agreed gently, truthfully. The landlord's wife arrived at the table with two bowls of soup and they began to eat.

'I've only really got to know him properly over the last five years or so,' Luke continued, obviously wanting to talk. 'My parents split up when I was very young, too young to know that my mother hated him, hated me, that she wanted to turn me against him.'

Laura was silent, not knowing what to say. She felt shocked. Had Tom's wife really tried to turn his son against him? It seemed incredible, horrific, yet why should Luke lie?

'You live with your mother?' she asked quietly, unable to contain her curiosity.

'I did, but I left as soon as I was old enough,' said Luke, his thin face harsh with remembered pain. 'I want to be with Tom.'

Laura concentrated on her soup, not wanting to ask him any more questions. It was obviously a painful subject and she had no right to pry, so she deliberately kept the conversation light and impersonal as they ate their main course of steak pie with deliciously-cooked vegetables and drank coffee.

At last they sat back warm and replete and Laura lit a cigarette. 'That was lovely,' she sighed pleasurably. 'Thanks for inviting me.'

'Thanks for giving in,' Luke replied wickedly, reminding her of her long prevarication.

'You can be very persuasive.' Her violet eyes were bright with laughter.

'I'm glad to hear that one of us can be.' The low cool voice behind her made Laura jump. She did not look round, but her whole body stiffened with awareness. Luke was laughing, pulling out a chair for Tom, and she watched covertly from beneath her lashes as he sat down next to her, gracefully coiling the long length of his body into the wooden seat.

'I'm sure if I asked Laura to draw breath she would suffocate herself rather than do as I asked,' Tom teased gently, the smile he flashed at her warm with charm.

Laura smiled despite herself, watching his eyes narrowing on her face. 'So complimentary,' she murmured softly, getting to her feet. She excused herself and headed quickly for the ladies' room, needing a few moments alone to pull herself together. What on earth was Tom doing here? she asked herself, examining herself in the mirror over the wash-basins. She looked awful, windswept, her eyes huge in her pale face, smudges of darkness beneath them. Awful. He was probably keeping an eye on Luke, making sure that Laura was not leading him on.

Shrugging defeatedly, she turned from the mirror and made her way back to the table. Tom was smoking idly, talking to Luke, and Laura watched them together as she approached. They were close, good friends more than father and son, and she felt a sharp stab of pain in the region of her heart. She did not want to be an outsider, she wanted to be part of their lives. And more than anything she wanted Tom. An impossible dream.

Both men rose as she sat down, charming, well-mannered, making her smile. Over drinks they talked impersonally, covering a wide range of topics from art to politics. Tom was warm and witty, yet Laura knew that he was watching her, watching Luke, assessing the situation between them with shrewd intelligence. She found herself falling deeply under the spell of his charm, actually relaxing, Luke acting as a kind of barrier between them—she had little doubt that had they been alone she and Tom would have been at each other's throats within five minutes.

An hour passed so quickly that she did not even notice, and it was only when her eye caught the clock on the wall that she realised the time. Grace would be wondering where she was.

With a fierce pang of regret she explained that she would have to leave. Surprisingly both men got to their feet ready to leave with her, despite her protests. Then they were in the Land Rover, Laura sandwiched between them, Tom's thigh hard and disturbing against hers in the cramped seats. As they drove back to the cottage she was jolted against him more than once, the car bumping violently down the tiny uneven roads, the hard touch of his body, however accidental, leaving her breathless, weak with longing for him. He steadied her, his hands gentle, almost caressing, and she avoided his eyes, not quite daring to look at him.

She knew that there was something wrong as soon as she stepped inside the cottage. Always sensitive to atmosphere, she could feel a tension, a weird sense of panic and unease. The lounge was deserted, as was the kitchen, but she could hear movement upstairs as she pulled off her boots and hung up her coat. She found Grace in the bedroom, her face pale and tear-stained, uncaringly throwing clothes into suitcases.

'Grace, what's happened? What's the matter?'

'It's Nick—I had a phone call,' Grace said in a sharp quick little voice. She did not turn round but carried on with her packing.

Laura frowned, walking into the room. 'What about Nick?' she demanded.

Grace turned then, a pile of hastily folded clothes falling unnoticed from her hands. 'Car accident,' she blurted, her eyes full of tears again. 'I have to go to him!'

Laura's eyes widened with pure shock. She took Grace gently by the shoulders and sat her down on the bed. 'Tell me about it,' she prompted quietly.

Grace reached for a tissue and dabbed at her eyes. 'Connie, Nick's secretary, telephoned about half an hour ago. He's in hospital, a pile-up on a motorway last night. It's serious, apparently—I *must* go!' she said in short distressed bursts.

'Oh no! How awful!' Laura muttered, wishing she could do something to help. 'Shall I look after the children?'

Grace shook her head. 'I'm taking them with me. They'll want to see him. If he . . . if he. . . . We have to be there.'

'Of course. Are you leaving straight away?' Grace

nodded, still fighting her tears. 'Shall I drive you down to London?'

'No, stay here. I want to go alone.' Grace's voice was sure and desperate.

'Are you sure?'

'Yes. Please stay Laura—I don't want to spoil your holiday. Please!'

Laura opened her mouth to protest, then shut it again. She did not want to upset Grace more by arguing over something unimportant, and in a way she was glad that Grace wanted her to stay. If she went back to London today she would find her flat invaded by strangers, and right now she needed peace. So she helped her friend pack and got the children organised for her, then made coffee, insisting that Grace sat down for five minutes before starting the journey.

Her friend seemed calm now, pale and composed. Christy and Jan, sensing something wrong, were quiet and subdued. Laura made up some sandwiches for their journey, knowing that Grace would not want to stop en route.

'Are you *sure* you don't want me to come with you?' she asked again as they loaded up the car. 'I could look after the children while you're at the hospital. I could help.'

But Grace would not be moved. 'No, Laura, I want you to stay. We'll all be staying at my mother's, there's no need to worry. Now go back inside before you get soaked to the skin.'

'Will you phone me?' Laura begged. 'Tonight or tomorrow?'

'I promise.' They hugged each other briefly and then Grace jumped into the car and was gone.

Laura walked slowly back inside, feeling worried and alone. I should have insisted, she told herself worriedly. Grace shouldn't be on her own. But when Grace made up her mind she was immovable. She had wanted to go alone and Laura could not have changed her mind.

The rain was still falling with heavy regularity, although the wind had died down a little. It was late afternoon and already dark. She switched on the lamps and stoked up the fire, still worrying about Grace. And she had just settled down with a cup of fresh coffee and a book when there was a loud banging on the door. Sighing, she went to answer it, but as her hand reached for the latch she realised how alone she was, how isolated. 'Who is it?' she called through the door, her voice tremulous.

'Tom—let me in,' came the deep brisk reply.

With suddenly trembling fingers Laura pulled open the door, her heart racing at the sight of him, lean and strong and very wet. In silence she stood back to let him in, their bodies brushing briefly in the tiny hallway. She found that she could not speak, her mouth was dry, there was a hard lump in her throat.

Tom was watching her, his cool grey eyes enigmatic, making her wholly aware of the tight jeans that clung to her rounded hips and her blue, figure-hugging tee-shirt. She pushed closed the front door and indicated the lounge. 'Please, go in,' she said lamely, her face very flushed. She did not want to go first, it would mean brushing past him again. She followed him into the lounge, staring at his gleaming wet hair, his wide shoulders and powerful back, and a fierce hunger filled her.

He turned and she lowered her eyes. 'Sit down. Would you like some coffee? I've just made some.'

Tom nodded. 'Yes, thank you.'

'Grace isn't here,' she rushed on. 'She's taken the children back to London.'

'I know.' His voice was low and calm. 'She rang me this afternoon.'

'Oh.' Surprised, Laura busied herself fetching another cup from the kitchen and pouring coffee. Tom watched her every movement. 'Will you be all right on your own?' he asked gently.

'I like being on my own,' she replied over-defensively.

He smiled. 'Okay—I didn't come here to fight.'

'Why did you come?'

'To make sure you could manage, to offer help.' His voice was flat and unemotional and Laura felt very silly.

'I'm sorry,' she said, lifting her hands gracefully. 'I've been very rude. But I'm worried about Grace. I wanted to go with her, but she said she wanted to go alone. I don't know whether or not I did the right thing.'

'You can only offer, you can't force people to accept help,' Tom said quietly.

'Yes, I know.' She watched him as he drank his coffee in two long mouthfuls, watched the muscles contracting in his throat. Why couldn't she talk to him normally? Why was it always so strained between them?

I don't want to be alone, she longed to say to him. Stay with me, don't leave me.

'*What?*' His head jerked upwards, eyes narrowing on her face, and she realised to her deep everlasting shame that she had been thinking aloud and had actually *asked* him not to leave her. She wanted to run, to hide, but his eyes held hers so fiercely that she could not even look away. Hot colour swamped her face and for a second she felt reckless, uncaring.

'Don't leave me,' she repeated on a whispered sigh.

Tom moved as though in slow motion, pulling her to her feet and holding her tightly, his cool mouth buried in the full softness of her hair. 'I have to,' he murmured heavily, rejecting her very gently. She buried her face against the damp material of his shirt, her body aching as she pressed herself against the hard warmth of him.

'I know that really,' she admitted in a muffled little voice.

'Oh, Laura, you drive me crazy!' he sighed, half exasperated, half serious, as he gently put her away from him.

'Do I?' Her eyes were bright, innocently provocative.

'You know damned well you do,' he said wryly, offering her a cigarette from the packet he took from his jacket pocket. He inhaled on his cigarette deeply. 'And I'm not the only one. Luke's been talking about you all afternoon,' he revealed bleakly, changing the subject.

Laura frowned, her brightness gone. 'That's not my fault!'

She did not want to talk about Luke. How could Tom be so hard, so cool? She felt so soft and weak after being in his arms for those brief moments.

'So why the hell did you agree to have lunch with him?' Tom demanded, his mouth an uncompromising line.

'I was tired,' she explained dully, feeling hurt by this sudden attack. 'I didn't know how to refuse and I didn't want to hurt him. Besides, I really don't see that it's any of your business,' she finished with a flash of her former spirit.

He turned away, his shoulders tense. 'No, you're

right, and I'm sorry,' he admitted surprising her.

'That's okay,' she replied immediately. 'It doesn't matter. Tom, I've never encouraged him. I like him, but . . . oh, well you know what I mean.' She was begging for his understanding, tired of all the tension, of all the arguments.

He looked at her, his grey eyes gentle. 'Yes, I know what you mean. God knows you're not responsible for his feelings—but I don't want him following in my footsteps, making the same goddamned mistakes I made.'

There was a harshness in his voice that almost frightened her. 'I don't understand—what mistakes?' she probed, knowing that to understand what he had said was very *very* important. But Tom shook his head, perhaps regretting his words. 'Forget it, little one, it's not important.' His tone brooked no argument, despite it's kindness, and Laura nearly stamped her foot with frustration. There was so much she didn't understand, so much unsaid, misunderstood between them. It was driving her insane!

'One of these days, Tom Farrell——' she threatened fiercely, her violet eyes dark with anger. 'Just you wait!'

He laughed, his teeth flashing in the tanned leaness of his face. 'I will be waiting, Laura,' he promised with deep significance. 'You can bet on it.'

Laura stared into his eyes, seeing flame leaping in the cool grey depths. She desperately wanted to go to him, to fling her arms around his waist and reveal her love for him. If she did that, though, it would do no good. He did not love her, she was as sure of that as she was of the interminable rain.

He did not want or need love. Brief affairs, lovers like Amanda Delvaux, they were all he needed, all he would ever need, and she knew that a brief affair with him—all he had to offer, as he himself had said—would destroy her, ruin her life with it's powerful shattering memories. And she realised that Tom knew that too. He desired her, but that was all, and he was not destructive or uncaring enough to take what he wanted, knowing what the consequences would be for her. He probably also knew that she loved him; she had never been any good at hiding her feelings, and his shrewd perception could not be denied. It was a rather humiliating thought, one that she instinctively backed away from as embarrassing and unacceptable.

In the silence Tom watched her, almost able to read her thoughts, her small face was so expressive. He took a pen from his pocket and wrote a number on the pad by the telephone.

'If you need any help, ring me. I want you to promise,' he said firmly.

'Help?' she echoed lamely, stung by his kindness because she wanted so much more.

'There may be flooding. If the rain keeps up the river will burst it's banks—it's running too high now— and I don't want you to be frightened or alone,' he explained calmly.

'I should have gone back to London,' Laura muttered sullenly.

'Yes, perhaps you should have. God knows why you came up here at this time of year—I warned Grace over and over about the flooding.'

To her over-sensitive ears he sounded cold and dismissive, as though he would have been glad to see the back of her. 'I would have gone back,' she began defiantly, wondering why she felt the need to explain herself to him. Useless to wonder, but she did. She certainly did not want to give him the impression that she had stayed because of him. He probably thought exactly that. With a shock of self-revelation she realised that it was true. She *had* stayed because of him, because he was here and because she was stupid and ridiculously hopeful. 'I would have, only. . . .'

'Only what?'

'My flat's full of people, Gino's friends from Italy.' Her voice was suddenly lost and very lonely.

Tom's mouth was suddenly tight. 'Is he coming here to see you?'

She nodded, inexplicably close to tears. 'Next weekend, probably. I hope so, I miss him.'

She did not notice the flare of anger in Tom's eyes. He put his hands on her shoulders and bending over he pressed his mouth tenderly to her forehead. 'He'll come,' he reassured her in a low harsh voice.

'I know.' She flashed him a smile, brilliant with faint hysteria. 'And you'd better go.'

Silently he nodded, moving indolently to the door. He looked back at her once, his expression dark and unfathomable, then he stepped outside and was gone. Laura locked the door behind him, moving mechanically, weighed down with a strong, strange sadness. She felt defeated by his concern, his kindness.

She wandered upstairs to her bedroom and stared out of the open window at the rain, straining her eyes against the murky darkness, searching without success for some trace of Tom.

She washed, then pulled off her clothes. She was exhausted, yet her body felt strangely alive, aching for his touch, his love. The cool silk of her nightdress slid softly over her heated skin. She switched out the light and slipped into bed. Tonight, despite the rain, there were patches of moonlight falling through the lace at the windows, lighting the room, illuminating the silver casket he had given her. It glowed in the darkness, mysterious, symbolic. It should have been given in love, she thought miserably, as she stared at it.

Slipping out of bed again, she lifted it from the chest of drawers, stroking the old smooth silver as she brought it to the bed. It was a part of him, the only part she had, except for her knowledge, and she wrapped her arms around it as she moved across the room.

Afterwards, she never knew what drew her once more to the window—some sixth sense, perhaps. Outside the rain was loud, the wind rising again. She knew she ought to shut the window, but she didn't want to, couldn't be bothered. She felt warm and safe and terribly alone.

Suddenly her heart skipped a beat, as her eyes, accustomed to the darkness now, picked out the tall shadow near the river. It was Tom. He was standing perfectly still, uncaring of the rain, it seemed, staring into the darkness. Laura stood and watched for long minutes, wondering why he stood there, while a vague sense of worry, of foreboding built up inside her.

Then, acting on impulse, she put down the casket and ran downstairs, pulling on her coat and boots and tugging open the front door. She did not know why, but she had to go to him.

He turned slowly as he heard her approaching, watching her through dark unreadable eyes as she reached his side. She stared into his face.

'What's the matter?' she asked quietly, her words almost lost in the wind.

'Go back inside.' His voice was harsh, the eyes holding hers shadowed with emotion.

She ignored that. 'Why are you standing here in the rain?'

'What the hell difference does it make' He was angry again.

Laura flinched. 'I . . . I thought there was something wrong. . . . I thought I could help. . . .' she faltered, wondering how she had found the courage to come out here in the first place.

Tom sighed, touching her hurt face gently. 'I'm sorry,' he said heavily. 'I was thinking about Luke.' There was a pause, then. 'You know Julia's dead?'

It was a bombshell, the very last thing she had expected. 'Dead?' she echoed in a hollow whisper, her heart stopping for a moment. What was he saying?

'Yes, dead.' His voice was flat, almost expressionless. 'Drowned—she was drunk. Luke's taking it badly, he can't even talk about it. He's hurt, but he's guilty for the way he felt about her, guilty about leaving her when he did. It's tearing him up.'

Laura stared at him, her mind crowded, buzzing with confused shocked thoughts. 'I didn't know. I'm sorry,' she whispered.

Tom shrugged. 'It only happened very recently. Luke didn't even know—that was one of the reasons I came up here.' He stared across the river, his face blank. 'I flew over to France as soon as I heard. Julia's father didn't even want Luke or myself at the funeral can you believe that?' His voice was rough with violence. 'His own grandchild!'

Laura did not understand, but her heart ached for him, for Luke.

'You must be very sad,' she said miserably, inadequately.

'Sad?' Tom turned to her curiously, as though he did not understand the word. 'No, not sad, little one. I feel pity maybe, nothing more. I didn't love her, and sixteen years is a long time—she was a stranger. My only concern is for Luke.' He lifted his powerful shoulders resignedly, wearily.

Laura frowned, terribly confused, terribly worried for him, yet relieved that it had not hurt him. She longed to help. She remembered what she had said to him in anger the day before, and felt like crying, and things that Luke had said about his mother over lunch, the pain and desperation she had sensed in him, suddenly seemed clear. It was like a nightmare. Tom's wife was dead and he could only feel pity. She would never understand.

Tom was staring at her. 'Go back inside,' he repeated gently. He did not need her help. Laura felt, irrationally, that he wanted her to go and turning from him, ran back to the loneliness of the house. She did not even notice that she was crying until she began to shake convulsively. Tom. Her heart cried out to him—and in her desperation she could not believe that he did not hear.

CHAPTER NINE

THREE continually rainy days later the river burst its banks and the cottage was badly flooded. On the morning of the day it happened, Laura woke late after yet another restless, haunted night.

She had not seen Tom since the night he had come to offer help, and had revealed the shocking news about his wife, but she had thought about him constantly, obsessively.

There had also been no sign of Luke. She felt worried about him, wondering how he was coping. Perhaps Tom had finally managed to warn him off, she thought, shocked by her own bitterness, her own pain, knowing that she was being terribly unfair.

Apart from the dreadful ache in her heart she was happy being alone. She was probably going quite mad, she often thought, wry and unconcerned, but she loved living in this cottage, loved its age, its clean air, its smallness.

When Grace had telephoned her two days before, sounding happier than Laura had heard her for months, Laura had not mentioned Julia's death. There was a curious shocked blankness inside her whenever she thought of it. She concentrated on Grace's news instead. Nick was still in hospital, having undergone surgery for some internal injuries, but he was slowly getting better, and it looked as though the divorce was off and the marriage on again. Nothing was finally settled, but Grace was very hopeful, very happy and obviously very much in love. Laura was thrilled, tearful with joy because Grace deserved happiness and it looked as though things were finally going to go right for her. Grace had asked about Tom and Laura had been vague, not mistaking the worry in her friend's voice. She had spent at least ten minutes reassuring Grace that she was fine, enjoying herself. And in a way it was true, she *was* enjoying herself—more than she would have done with the same problems in London.

That day she took a leisurely bath before breakfast and decided to go for a long walk. She was getting quite used to the constant rain, in fact she could hardly remember any other weather. She laughed softly as she pulled on her boots, recalling how she had scoffed at Luke's predictions of flood. It seemed like years ago, but in reality was only a week. It had been hot and sunny then. Incredible!

She walked all day, a habit she had easily fallen into. It was lonely and enjoyable and it helped her sleep at nights. Finding herself in the village around midday, she had her lunch at the pub where Luke had taken her. The landlord and his wife remembered her and she enjoyed chatting with them over her meal.

By the time she got back to the cottage she was worn out and it was dark and very wet; the water was up past her ankles, almost to her knees. When she realised that the cottage was flooded, faint panic stirred inside her. She had no idea what to do. There was no electricity, which was frightening, but she remembered a torch in the kitchen, wading through the high water to get it.

Tom. He had left his number; she would ring him and he would know what to do. But her heart sank as she picked up the receiver. The telephone was as dead as the power supply. She tried dialling and pressing

the little black buttons on top of the phone, her panic
increasing as the cold facts hit her. She was totally
isolated, miles from anywhere, without heat, light or
communication and the cottage, usually so friendly and
welcoming suddenly seemed menacing, a prison. She
should have gone back to London when she had the
chance, she was crazy to have stayed alone. Absolutely
crazy. She had been warned of the floods, but had
thought she would be able to cope. Now she knew
better. If only the cottage had not been so isolated, so
far from the nearest village, she would not have been
so frightened.

How high would the water rise? She could die here
and nobody would find her for months. She recognised
her own hysteria and tried to calm herself down, her
eyes straining in the darkness, noticing shadows that
she could not recognise, flashing the torch quickly and
fearfully into the corners of the room. She shivered
violently. It was cold without the fire and she could
not even make herself a hot drink to warm herself up.
Splashing through the dirty water, she made her way
upstairs with some difficulty. It was cold and pitch-
black, the only sound the rain and the faint bangings
and creakings of the old building. It was frightening.

She sat down on her bed and wondered what to do,
huddled in the blankets for warmth. She could stay in
the cottage for the night, she supposed. There was
nothing she could do tonight, perhaps tomorrow, when
it was light, she could try and sort something out.

A loud crashing noise from downstairs made her
jump and she froze with fear, her ears straining to hear.
Had she locked the front door? She couldn't remember. What if there was somebody prowling around
downstairs? Her heart missed a beat, then began to
hammer as the imagination she could not control ran

riot. Nobody would hear her if she screamed. There was nobody to come to her rescue. And she could hear other noises now, a faint scratching sound, a low creaking, as though. . . .

She released her caught breath, her lungs tight and painful, her fingers so tight around the torch that they ached, her knuckles white. She stared towards the open doorway, expecting at any second to see someone, something, entering the room. She couldn't stay here, she just *couldn't*! Her nerves were already stretched to breaking point, she would not manage to survive the night alone. Inspiration struck. She would go to Tom's cottage. She knew what direction it was in, vaguely knew the shortcut Luke had shown her. She only hoped she could find it in the dark. She grabbed the silver casket, knowing that she could not leave it behind, just in case there *was* somebody in the cottage, and flung it, together with her handbag, into a larger bag which she slid over her shoulders so that her hands were free.

She was ready to go, and her next problem was how to brave going downstairs alone. There was a cold film of perspiration on her face as she crept towards the door, fear making her stomach empty, her heart thud sickeningly. It's all in your imagination, she kept telling herself sternly, but it was no good. She was firmly caught in her own fear like a fly in a spider's web and there was no escape. Taking a deep breath, she braced herself and crept downstairs keeping the torch off. If there was somebody there she did not want to attract their attention. All she wanted to do was to get out of the cottage unscathed and in one piece.

It was quiet, the silence ringing in her ears louder than bells, and she could imagine an intruder crouching in the darkness waiting for her. She licked her dry lips nervously and took another step downwards. Suddenly a window banged shut in the wind, its noise reverberating through the silent house. It was the last straw, and Laura shot down the remaining stairs as though she was being hunted, splashing through the water that seemed even deeper now, towards the front door, which she found, as she had feared, unlocked.

Once outside she turned and made her way in the direction of Tom's house. She fell more than once and was soaked from head to toe within minutes. If she got on to higher ground it might be easier, she realised, trying to find the road. So she began to climb, the deep mud hampering her, feeling desperate and achingly tired after walking all day. She had no idea where she was going, with only a vague idea of the right direction. The torch was practically useless and she needed both her hands to keep her balance.

She stopped suddenly, exhausted tears pouring down her face, indistinguishable from the rain. It came to her then that she probably should have stayed in the cottage. At least she would have been dry and relatively safe. As it was, she had the feeling she was already lost. But however crazy it was, she felt that there was no way she could go back. No way.

She climbed a little higher and to her relief found a road, stumbling on to it by chance but with great relief. She had no idea whether it was the right road, but she had to take a chance. She tried to decide which direction to take and chose the one she thought led to Tom's cottage. If she got to him she would be safe. It was the only certainty that kept her going.

She trudged along for about half an hour, using the torch to light her way, profoundly glad that she was above the worst of the flooding at last—it was a step in the right direction, she thought with a weak smile. She was getting accustomed to the darkness now, her eyesight sharpening as she concentrated hard on putting one tired leg in front of the other, so as she rounded a sharp bend she was unprepared for the blaze of headlights that suddenly blinded her.

The car was almost upon her. She stood confused and transfixed in the middle of the road. Afterwards she could not understand why she had not heard its approach, but she remembered with painful clarity standing in the road, paralysed, unable to move a muscle, certain that she would be killed. They had come upon each other so quickly around that dangerous bend, there was no time for the driver to even sound the horn. There was a terrifying screaming of brakes, and the car missed her by mere inches, skidding on the wet road and crashing into a ditch. Laura stood perfectly still for a moment and as reaction set in, began to shake, not daring to look at the car to her left, certain that the driver had been killed.

As though in a dream she heard the slam of a door, then hard fingers closed on her shoulders dragging her round full circle so that she was staring into the violently angry face of Tom Farrell, who, incredibly, seemed unhurt.

He shook her so hard that her teeth seemed to rattle. 'You bloody stupid, crazy little fool!' he grated, almost beyond control. 'What the hell do you think you're doing out here?'

Laura stared at him in silence, dazed and very confused. It was all too much for her—the floods, the fear, the accident and now Tom's anger, and she began to cry in earnest, her slender body shaking beneath his hands.

Tom swore violently, her tears angering him even more. 'For God's sake stop crying!' he snapped, his fingers tightening on the frail bones of her shoulders as though he would snap them.

His harsh uncompromising words reached something proud and angry inside her and she made a visible effort to pull herself together. 'Don't be angry,' she whispered between long shaking sobs.

'What the hell do you expect? You nearly killed us both!' he almost shouted, his eyes glittering savagely on her pale tragic face.

'I'm sorry,' she sniffed pathetically.

He stared down at her for a moment, then sighed, touching her face gently. 'Dammit, Laura, I thought I was going to hit you—you scared the hell out of me!' His anger was dissolving with a great deal of self-control.

'Are you hurt?' she asked worriedly, calmer now. She had found him, she was with him, and that was all that mattered, all her fear and discomfort were forgotten, eased away by his strong, albeit furious presence and relief that he was not injured.

'No, I'm not hurt—the car looks like a write-off, though.' They walked over to it, both oblivious of the pelting rain. It was nose down in the ditch, the windscreen shattered, obviously damaged, obviously immovable; there was no way they were going to get it moving on a night like this without help.

'I'm so sorry,' Laura repeated, feeling responsible.

'Stop apologising,' Tom ordered quite mildly, and slid with difficulty through the passenger door, the only access into the driver's seat, and as Laura watched, tried to start the engine. There was no response apart from a sharp metallic tearing sound. He tried again with the same result, then, still swearing under his breath, climbed out of the car. 'Nothing,' he muttered through clenched teeth, his fist slamming down on to the car roof.

Laura was silent, her body drooping with exhaustion as she stared at him. He was as wet as she was, she realised, clothes clinging uncomfortably to his tense powerful body.

'What will we do?' she asked wearily, utterly confident that he would know.

He shook his dark head, thinking hard. 'We can't stay in the car, we'd probably freeze to death, and the rain is already coming in on the far side through the windscreen.'

'Your house?' she queried miserably.

His eyes slid over her, noting her extreme tiredness, her weakness. 'Too far and too dangerous, you'd never make it, little one. And to get back to either cottage would mean going back down into the flooded area. We can't take that risk in the dark, the water will be rising higher all the time.'

A thought struck her. 'Luke! Where's Luke?' she asked in panic, gripping at his arm.

'Don't worry, he drove to Edinburgh this morning to visit a friend. I don't think he'll be back tonight, and even if he is he'll have more sense than to go to the cottage,' Tom replied calmly, allaying her fears. He reached into the car again and pulled a blanket from the back seat and a small silver flask from the glove compartment. Then he took her hand. 'Come on.'

'Where?' Her legs were obeying him even as she asked.

'There's an old empty crofter's cottage not far from here. We can spend the night there. We don't really have much choice, it's bloody impossible to do anything else tonight.'

So Laura clung to his hand, accepting his help as they climbed further up off the road and ten minutes later they were at the dilapidated cottage. Tom forced open the door with his shoulder and pulled her inside. It was dark and smelled very damp and musty, but at least it was dry and solid and, as yet, not flooded. 'Wait here and don't move,' he ordered as he took the torch and disappeared. She did as she was told, staring into the darkness with blind eyes, listening to the noises of him moving about, her mind almost blank with the shock of the evening's events.

Tom returned within five minutes, actually smiling. 'It's okay—there's an old mattress and enough rotten timber for a fire—not exactly the Ritz, but we'll be fine.'

He took her hand again and led her through the darkness. Laura stood and watched, holding the torch for him as he gathered wood and lit a fire in the small iron grate. She watched the easy graceful movements of his body as he worked, her mind slowly clearing. She felt *so* cold, but the fire was bright now and warm, and getting bigger by the minute.

Tom passed her the silver flask. 'Drink,' he ordered gently. 'It will make you warm.

She took a tentative mouthful and coughed as it burned the back of her throat. 'It's horrible! I hate brandy,' she whispered.

He laughed. 'It's good for you.' His hand reached out and touched her face. 'God, you're freezing!' He handed her the blanket. 'Get out of those wet clothes and wrap yourself in this.' He saw her obvious hesitation and his mouth twisted impatiently. 'Laura, for God's sake, this is no time for modesty—you're going to catch pneumonia if you don't get out of those clothes.'

She stared at him defiantly. 'Will you please turn your back?' He lit a cigarette and turned away. She watched him for a moment, then tried to pull off her coat. It felt as though it was glued to her body and her arms, heavy, numb and tired, would not move to her brain's commands. So she stood still, her eyes on Tom's wide shoulders until he said, 'Are you respectable yet?'

She sighed. 'I can't manage,' she admitted in a very small voice, dreadfully embarrassed because she had to ask for his help.

He flung his cigarette into the fire and turned towards her, his lean face unreadable. 'Shall I do it for you, little one?'

She nodded in silence, her face running with hot colour.

His hands were quick and gentle as he stripped off her soaking clothes, his face blank and impersonal, and when she stood before him pale and silent, her head lowered, in only her brief lacy underwear, he pulled the blanket around her, his fingers accidentally brushing her bare skin, making her shiver, and sat her down on the mattress he had dragged near to the fire, ordering her to take another sip of brandy. With pleasure she could feel the warmth gradually seeping back into her limbs.

'What about your clothes?' she demanded worriedly.

He shrugged, pulling off his jacket and shirt, his broad naked chest gleaming in the firelight. 'As we only have one blanket that's about the best I can do,' he said dryly, lowering himself down on to the mattress beside her. He indicated the bag he had pulled from her shoulders. 'What's that?'

Laura smiled selfconsciously. 'You wouldn't believe it.'

'Try me,' he invited teasingly. She opened the bag and pulled out the silver casket.

Tom laughed softly, not unkindly, his grey eyes meeting hers. 'Oh, Laura, Laura!' His voice was amused, very tender. She blushed and looked away, suddenly very aware of him, half naked beside her, very aware of the isolated intimacy of their surroundings.

He lit two cigarettes and handed one to her. 'Tell me how you came to be on the road.'

She drew on her cigarette. 'I was out walking all day and when I got back the cottage was flooded, so quickly—I couldn't believe it—no phone, no electricity. I thought I could manage upstairs.' She shuddered in remembrance. 'But it was too dark, too frightening, and I ran looking for you. I didn't mean to cause that accident—honestly. I didn't hear you or see you until it was too late.' She bit her lip, her eyes beseeching.

Tom slid an arm around her shoulders and hugged her. 'It doesn't matter, I swear to you it doesn't. It's insured, so don't worry. I'm only glad that I didn't hit you.'

'Where were you going?' she asked curiously.

'Would you believe, to see you?' He smiled at her surprise. 'I thought you'd gone back to London, I've been telephoning and I called once or twice, but the place was always empty. Then when the river burst its banks I thought I'd better make sure, so I telephoned your flat. I spoke to Premoli, who told me you were still here. I was worried, so I drove over,' he explained briefly.

Laura felt a rush of happiness at his concern and without thinking of the consequences she leaned over and pressed her mouth to his hard cheek in a brief kiss. 'Thank you for caring,' she said quietly, regretting her impulsive action as she felt the slight stiffening of his body.

'Somebody has to,' he told her wryly. 'You don't seem able to look after yourself.'

That made her laugh. 'Thanks very much!' But she felt happy, warm and rather drowsy from the heat, the brandy.

Her hair was drying fast, a soft golden halo around her small face. 'Do you get flooded every year?' she asked.

'No, every couple of years—it's the position of the cottages in the valley. The local people have been talking about floods for months. I told Grace, but she wanted to get away—crazy to come here at this time of year.'

Laura told him about Grace and Nick and their hopes for a new start. 'And anyway,' she finished defensively, 'you're here.'

'I know what I'm doing.'

'And Luke?'

Tom shrugged his powerful shoulders. 'Luke needed some peace, some time alone. His life has been pretty rough lately——' He broke off abruptly as though he felt he had said too much.

'He's so like you,' Laura said dreamily, not pushing it.

Tom smiled. 'Thank you.'

'And I'm so tired,' she murmured, realising that he still had his arm around her.

'So go to sleep,' he said laughingly, moving so that she could lie down. She watched him as she lay sleepily wrapped tightly in the blanket. He collected more wood and built up the fire, then hung out their clothes above it so that they would dry during the night.

He had looked after her so well tonight, she could almost believe that he cared for her. She drifted into a light sleep almost immediately, her body warm and relaxed, safe in the knowledge that he was with her and so nothing could go wrong.

She woke with a start, some hours later, cold and frightened. She lay perfectly still for a moment, her eyes wide, her heart beating fast, loudly in her ears, as she remembered where she was, what had happened. Then she rolled over and saw Tom. He was squatting near the fire, smoking, his face a hard blank mask, his eyes unfathomable as he stared into the flames. There was an air of stillness about him. In silence Laura watched the heavy muscles of his shoulder and arm tensing as he lifted the cigarette to his lips, watched the firelight flickering on his smooth bare skin, on his broad hair-roughened chest, and desire swept through her, a fierce warm ache in her stomach, her legs, her breasts.

'Tom. . . .' She whispered his name and he turned his head slowly, his eyes darkening as he looked at her. 'I'm so cold and so frightened.' Her voice trembled.

He flung his cigarette into the flames with an easy cat-like grace that riveted her attention. 'Come closer to the fire,' he said, and there was a soft roughness in his voice.

'Won't you hold me?' she begged achingly. He did not move, his body tensing, his eyes holding hers. 'Please. . . .' she whispered. He muttered something violent under his breath, but moved towards her, strong and graceful, his brown hands reaching for her. She twisted so that he could wrap himself in the blanket as he took her half naked body into his arms, lying beside her now, holding her tightly.

His body was hard and warm and she clung to him, shivering as much with desire as with cold. His hands lay flat against her bare spine, the metal buckle of his belt digging in to the soft skin of her stomach. She laid her head against his shoulder with a small sigh of contentment.

'Go back to sleep,' he ordered harshly. 'Yes,' she murmured obediently, sliding her slim arms around him. 'And for God's sake lie still,' he added in a low hard voice, his body tensing beneath her hands.

She laughed softly, warm now and not at all frightened. 'Are you going to sleep?'

'I damned well hope so,' he replied very dryly. She laughed again, turning her face into his smooth skin, her nostrils filling with his clean male scent, and fell back to sleep almost immediately.

When she woke again it was dawn. She could hear the birds singing sweetly outside. She stretched languidly against Tom's hard body, knowing the joy of waking in the arms of the man she loved. She opened her eyes slowly and looked up at him, to find that he was already awake, staring down at her, his grey eyes dark, warm and very serious.

He had been awake for an hour, watching her as she slept like a baby in his arms. 'Good morning.' His voice was deep, husky, his mouth smiling.

Laura blushed furiously. 'Has . . . has the fire gone out?' she said lamely, wondering why she asked.

'Yes, hours ago.' He sounded uncaring, one of his hands stroking her golden hair out of her face, his long fingers soothing, gentle. That hot aching weakness was in her again as he touched her, and she nestled closer, feeling a sweet triumph at the acceleration of his heartbeat beneath the palm of her hand.

How she loved him, how she wanted him! Nothing in the world mattered except being near him, and she wanted to know his lovemaking just once before she let him go. He was the only man she would ever love, she knew that with a deep inner certainty, and the fact that he did not love her, the fact that she would probably never be as close to him again, made her desperate to experience making love with the one man she would always want. She wanted to give him her virginity, the priceless gift of her innocence, because it already belonged to him and because she would never want anybody else.

She wanted to know him, wanted him to become her lover. She needed him and she needed him now, so she lifted her head and kissed his mouth, hearing him draw breath harshly as though she had flicked him with a whip. For a second he did not respond to the innocent sweetness of her kiss. Love me, she begged silently; I belong to you already, you must know that. She pulled away and stared into his face. There was a muscle jerking in his jaw, the eyes that held hers were almost black, unsmiling.

'Laura. . . .' he said huskily, very softly.

'Make love to me,' she said desperately, very clearly. 'Show me. . . .'

He closed his eyes as though fighting some cruel inner battle, and she stared at the dark lashes against his tanned cheek with wonder. Reaching up, she touched his face. It was rough beneath her fingers. A second later he groaned, his mouth finding hers, parting her lips hungrily, his kiss exploding through her body, setting fire to her skin, her blood. He moved, lithe and fast, one swift easy movement, so that she lay beneath him, the hard tense weight of his body pressing her into the mattress with an urgency that weakened her.

She began to tremble as she drowned beneath the pleasure of his mouth, his kiss deepening, feeding on her response, deeper and deeper more hungry, more demanding. She could feel his hands slowly stroking over the curves of her body, their touch light and sensual. His mouth left hers, travelling over her face, brief tender kisses trailed over her forehead, cheeks and chin, and down to her throat, pressing his lips to the pulse that beat so frantically there. Laura arched back her head in weak submission, her hands at his wide bare shoulders. Deftly he unclipped her bra, his fingers stroking over her swelling, tautening breasts. She moaned as he touched her, caught by a boiling hot fever that set her blood racing round her body. His mouth was flame at her shoulders, at her breasts, his hands still stroking, exploring.

He made love to her slowly, expertly, patiently arousing her until she was shuddering beneath his hands, beneath his lips. Her hands were moving too, over his muscled arms, the roughness of the hair that matted his chest. She kissed his shoulders, tasting the smooth sweat-dampened skin, feeling him shaking as she touched him.

Then his mouth parted hers again and she realised that he was as naked as she was, his hard rough thigh parting hers, his body against her, strong and tense and urgent. His fingers were moving on her skin again, and she was lost, crying out his name when the pleasure became so intense that she could hardly bear it.

Tom moved over her then, murmuring her name, murmuring deep endearments into her mouth, his breathing harsh and uneven as he finally possessed her. Laura writhed beneath the slow thrusting invasion of his powerful body. All thought was lost to her, she knew only his strength, his energy, the heat of him, and she clung to him blindly as he finally brought them both to a mindless overpowering climax.

Afterwards he rolled on to his back and took her

into his arms, gently pushing back her hair from her damp forehead. Laura lay against his hard body, feeling his heart hammering against her breasts. She was exhausted, fulfilled and languorously satisfied. Making love, becoming Tom's lover, had been more shattering, more beautiful than she had ever imagined. She wanted to think, wanted to talk, but her eyes were drooping, sensual lethargy curling her body against his in total relaxation. Tom smiled down at her, his grey eyes strangely glazed, and touched his mouth tenderly to her forehead. She was falling asleep, drifting away on a cloud of pleasure, the last thing she was consciously aware of being Tom's arms tightening around her.

She never knew what woke her, but as she opened her eyes she was aware that something was going on. Something was wrong. Tom was alert and very still beside her, and as she lifted her head from his shoulder she saw Luke tensed in the doorway of the empty room, his eyes riveted on their entwined bodies, his expression lost and angry.

She looked at Tom. He was staring at his son, but he did not get the chance to say a word. Luke muttered something under his breath and whirled from the room, his footsteps hurried, echoing on the stone floor.

Tom sighed heavily, already on his feet. 'I have to go after him, he's hurt and angry.'

'Yes, I know.' Her eyes were miserable on his magnificent body as he dressed with fast careless grace.

He knelt beside her, his eyes dark and tormented. 'Laura, we have to talk.' She nodded mutely. 'I'll find Luke and then I'll be back. Wait for me?' He was searching her face, talking urgently. She nodded again, her throat closed, speechless for some strange reason. Tom bent over her and kissed her mouth. 'Wait for me.' A second later he was gone.

Fortunately her clothes were dry and she dressed immediately, wishing that she could wash, longing for a hot shower. As it was, she could only splash her face and hands in cold water from the rain-barrel. Incredibly it wasn't raining today, the sky was a grey, dirty blue. Laura stared out over the valley; it was shrouded in mist, nothing to be seen at all. She felt strangely uneasy; the feeling had been nagging away at her ever since she had seen Luke. How on earth had he found them? Tom had told her that his son was in Edinburgh. Luke must have found the damaged car on the road and searched for them.

Even now she could remember the expression in Luke's eyes as he looked at them, it made her wince. She sat down on the mattress and pulling a brush from her handbag tried to restore some order to her tousled hair. What have I done? she asked herself miserably. In the cold light of day her behaviour seemed appalling, humiliating and her face ran with colour. She had begged him to make love to her. He had resisted at first, but she had used her physical power over him, knowing that he desired her, to force the issue.

There was a weakness in her stomach even now as she remembered his fierce exultant lovemaking. No doubt last night would reinforce his low opinion of her morals, and she was sure, so sure, that he would know how she loved him. She had just added herself to the long list of Tom Farrell's easy conquests, setting herself up to be hurt.

Somewhere, probably London, Amanda Delvaux waited for him, and Laura had merely been a pleasant, unexpected interlude in his life. She was certain, would have staked her life on the fact that he did not love her. So what did they have to talk about? Why had he asked her to wait for him? If she did wait, she had the feeling that she would be so embarrassed she would want to die. She could never be a part of Tom's life, never. The best thing she could do would be to get away and try to put him out of her mind for ever.

She looked back on their brief stormy relationship. He had been kind and he had desired her. But he had also told her honestly that he could only offer her an affair, and after a night spent in his arms she knew that a brief affair would destroy her, when the end came. She should have got away when she had the chance. As it was, it was probably too late; the memory of last night would haunt her all her life, ruining her chances of a relationship with anybody else.

A hot rush of tears scalded her face. What had she done? It was sheer self-destruction, and she made a sudden decision.

She collected the silver casket and her handbag and walked out of the cottage, away from Tom, away from everything they had shared. She might have acted foolishly, but she had some instinct of self-preservation left, and all her instincts told her to run.

CHAPTER TEN

LATE the next day Laura arrived back in London. She had been remarkably lucky. On leaving the crofter's cottage, she had walked in the direction of the village and a car had stopped for her. It had been the landlord of the pub in the village. He had given her a lift to the village and his wife had run her to the nearest town, after hearing about the flooded cottage. Laura had bought some clothes and checked into a hotel, where she had spent the afternoon in a hot bath.

The morning after, she had hired a car and driven home. It was a relief to be home and luckily there was no sign of Gino or his Italian friends. As she made coffee and wandered round the flat her time in Scotland became dreamlike, unreal. This flat and her life in London, they were her realities. She wanted much more.

She slept for the rest of the afternoon and evening, exhausted after the long drive. The telephone woke her at nine o'clock that night.

'Laura?' It was Tom, and he sounded angry. Her heart pounded heavily and her hand, gripping the receiver, trembled.

'Yes?' She strove to keep her voice cool.

'Where the hell have you been? I've been out of my mind with worry!' His low voice grated with anger, shivering down her spine.

'Well, there's no need to worry, I've come home and I'm fine,' she said with shaky calmness.

He swore violently. 'Why didn't you wait for me?'

'I didn't want to. . . .' Her voice was becoming defiant, as she fought her urge to admit everything to him. 'I can't talk now . . . I'm sorry.' She replaced the receiver quickly, near to tears.

The phone rang again almost immediately and she ignored it, blocking the sound from her ears with her hands as she paced the room. Why couldn't he leave her alone? She could not take any pressure from him. If he used his charm and his persuasive powers, she would crumble. She *had* to keep him at arm's length. As soon as the ringing stopped, she snatched up the receiver and left it off the hook.

The next morning she met Gino on the stairs as she went out for a walk. He was alone.

'Where are your friends? I expected to find my flat full of them.' She managed a smile, but it was an effort.

He shrugged mournfully. 'Air traffic controllers' strike in Rome. They won't be here until next week now.' His eyes slid over her from head to toe, shrewdly assessing. 'I wasn't expecting you either.'

'The cottage is flooded out—no point in staying on.' Her cheeks were hot.

He nodded. 'Farrell has been on the phone more than once,' he said, not bothering to be casual.

'I know, he told me.' Laura sounded as miserable as she felt, and Gino touched her cheek.

'Anything I can do, baby?' There was a dark air of resignation about him. He knew, of course, that she loved Tom, she was branded with her sadness, her love. It was not as easy to let her go as he had thought it would be.

'There's nothing anybody can do, but thanks anyway. I suppose I'll get over it.'

As she walked in the park she began to think clearly. She might have been able to put the phone down on Tom, but that was because he was far away—at least she assumed he was still in Scotland. As soon as he got back to London it would be a different story. If he chose to pursue her, she would not have a chance. Tom Farrell was the sort of man who always got what he wanted, who let nothing stand in his way. If she wanted to avoid him, and for her own peace of mind she needed to, she would have to get away from the flat. After all, that was the first place he would look.

Laura racked her brains, wondering where to go; somewhere he would not think of looking, if he was looking at all, and she could think of no good reason why he should. She came up with Joss's house. He was away, so if she could contact him in Italy she could ask for the use of his house. She sighed. It was all so ridiculous, her life was upside-down, a total wreck, and she was on the run, all because she couldn't face the man she loved.

Perhaps when she'd had a few days peace and safety she would have sorted out her ravaged emotions and would be able to face him, pretend that she didn't care, tell him once and for all that she did not want to see him. But right now she was too confused, too vulnerable and too ashamed of what she had done.

Getting the number of Joss's apartment in Rome was not easy, but she finally managed it, and fortunately he did not ask a lot of questions, perhaps hearing the urgency, the unveiled desperation in her voice. He told her that she could use the house for as long as she needed and gave her the address and telephone number of his sister, who had a spare set of keys. He would ring his sister immediately and explain the situation in advance. Laura couldn't thank him enough.

Half an hour later everything was arranged, and with an ever-increasing sense of urgency she flung some essentials and, crazily, the silver casket, into a suitcase and went to find Gino to explain. He was out, his door firmly locked, so she scribbled a hasty note reassuring him, but not revealing where she was going, and shoved it under his door, then she left, stepping into the waiting taxi with pure relief.

Joss's house was enormous, furnished luxuriously with antiques and modern art. Laura felt almost lost in the huge ornate rooms, but it was a refuge, one she badly needed, she felt safe, and in consequence slept quite well that night.

The following afternoon she was forced out of the protective shell of the house into the outside world, shopping for food. Walking down Oxford Street, purposely chosen for its busyness, happy to lose herself in the crowds and wander round in the open air, she literally bumped into Amanda Delvaux.

Incredibly the Frenchwoman smiled. 'Hello, Laura.' She looked ravishingly beautiful in cream tweed and gold jewellery.

'Hello.' Laura could not help her lack of enthusiasm. It was sheer jealousy, she acknowledged miserably. Amanda Delvaux was, after all, living in Tom's house, obviously his lover. This woman had everything Laura wanted. She moved to walk past the other woman, but Amanda Delvaux lightly caught her arm.

'Have you time for a coffee?' she asked with a charming smile.

Laura almost gasped, pulling herself together, just in time. 'No . . . no, not really,' she replied, glancing at her watch and trying to give the impression that she was in a frantic hurry. 'I . . . er. . . .'

'Oh, please, surely you have ten minutes. I really

would like to talk to you.' Laura was lost for words, wondering what on earth was going on, and the next moment found herself being guided towards a small restaurant. She suddenly realised exactly what was happening. She was about to be warned off.

Amanda Delvaux ordered two coffees and they sat down at a table near the window. The Frenchwoman pulled out a packet of cigarettes from her expensive leather handbag and offered one to Laura.

'You said you wanted to talk to me,' Laura began uncertainly, waiting for the explosion. She supposed she deserved it.

'Yes, I want to talk about Tom,' Amanda Delvaux replied without preamble, her blue eyes sharpening on Laura's face which was suddenly suffused with colour. 'I have no wish to interfere—but I can tell, merely by looking at you, that you love him. . . .'

'Please—I don't want to talk about Tom,' Laura cut in quickly and rather desperately. 'I can assure you that I won't be seeing him again—you don't understand——'

'I think I do.' The Frenchwoman's eyes were kind. 'You can tell me to mind my own business if you like, but Tom's a good friend and I can't bear to see him the way he is at the moment.'

Friend? Laura almost laughed. She probably would have done if she hadn't been so close to tears. Anxiety seeped into her mind. 'The way he is at the moment?' she echoed weakly. 'What do you mean?'

'He returned from Scotland yesterday. As you know, Yves and I are staying with him. His mood is black— he is so angry, so restless—he's tearing himself apart trying to find you.'

Laura was hardly listening. 'Yves?' she demanded, her mind spinning. '*Yves?*' She was aware of how rude she was being, but she could not help herself. This was very, *very* important.

'My husband,' Amanda Delvaux explained with a faint shrug of her slim shoulders, then as she read Laura's eyes, her own widened with surprise. 'You surely did not think. . . ?'

'I did,' Laura admitted, feeling foolish.

Amanda Delvaux laughed. 'It's an interesting idea, Tom is quite a man—but I love my husband. The three of us are old friends, going back many years. Yves is in London on business and Tom invited us to stay at his home, it is as simple as that.'

Laura wanted to shout with joy. How could she have been so blind, so untrusting? How could she have thought such dreadful things about Tom? She remembered the dark, foreign-looking man who had been at the party with Amanda Delvaux and Tom. Yves.

'You must forgive me, Madame Delvaux,' she said apologetically.

'Amanda, please?'

'Amanda is one of my favourite names,' Laura smiled.

'My grandmother was English,' the Frenchwoman explained. 'All my sisters have English names.' She got to her feet. 'Excuse me, I must powder my nose, as they say here in England.'

Alone at the table, Laura sipped her coffee thoughtfully. Jumping to conclusions had always been one of her faults, but this time she had overreached herself. Amanda Delvaux and Tom had never been lovers. She was a happily married woman, and that meant that Tom was not the cold-hearted philanderer Laura had thought him to be. He had not been pursuing Laura while his mistress waited for him at his home. It had all been in her mind. It was an illusion she had deliberately created to try and squash her fragile, frightening love for him. Had she really been so afraid of being hurt? Thinking of him, she felt her heart contract with love. None of this changed the fact that he did not love her, nor the fact that she had behaved so very badly and could not face him.

Amanda Delvaux appeared at the table again, flawless and very beautiful. 'Would you like more coffee?' she asked as she sat down. 'I'm going to order some more, shopping always makes me so very thirsty.'

'Thank you.' Smiling at Amanda, Laura knew that she had found a new and unexpected friend. Crazy to think that ten minutes before she had been ready to scratch the other woman's eyes out. 'Amanda, I really do want to apologise, I've been terribly rude to you. You see, I'm afraid I . . . well, I rather jumped to conclusions when I saw you at Tom's house, and to be perfectly honest I was jealous. I hope you can forgive me, I hope that we can be friends.'

Amanda smiled. 'I am sure we will be friends. After all, we do already have a mutual friend.'

'Tom isn't my friend,' Laura said sadly. 'I think I've ruined everything.'

But Amanda shook her burnished head. 'Tom will not let you ruin everything.'

'I don't understand. . . .'

'I've known Tom for years, his life has been hard, uncompromising, cruel. Julia, his wife, she was cold and spiteful—he had no life with her, she gave him nothing, even tried to take his son from him. Now, thank God, he is finally free of her, he has Luke, and he has waited too many years for the right woman. I think he may almost be afraid to reach out for something good, something beautiful, but I happen to think, judging by his mood lately, that you are the woman he has been waiting for. I hope so. He needs somebody like you.' Her eyes were kind and sad and sincere.

'I'd like to think so,' Laura said wistfully. 'But I can't believe it, however hard I try.' Her head suddenly jerked upwards, her eyes widening. Tom was entering the restaurant, striding towards their table with angry, cat-like grace, his face a cold, furious mask.

'Now it is my turn to apologise,' Amanda said ruefully. 'I telephoned Tom and told him you were here.'

'Oh!' Laura was lost for words, her mind not taking in the small betrayal, her eyes riveted on the man moving towards them.

Then Tom was by her side, his eyes burning as he pulled her to her feet, oblivious to the curious looks being cast in their direction by other diners. 'You're coming with me,' he said harshly. 'And I'm not arguing.' He turned, and flashed a tight smile at Amanda Delvaux. 'Excuse us?'

'Of course.' Her smile was sweet.

'Now just a minute——' Laura began, the touch of his fingers beneath her elbow disturbing her, making her heart beat faster.

'I've told you I'm not going to argue with you, Laura, so shut up!' He was already propelling her out of the restaurant.

She glared at him. 'Let me go!' she muttered through her teeth, but he ignored her. 'I said let. . . .'

'I heard what you said.' He halted for a moment, staring down at her golden head, his grey eyes glittering dangerously. 'Do you want to make a scene? Go ahead,' he invited coolly. Laura glanced at the turned heads, the avid eyes, and her colour rose. 'Well?' he prompted.

'Where are we going?' she demanded, her face sullen.

'Somewhere we can talk,' he replied impassively.

Laura shrugged. She did not understand why he was so angry.

She let him lead her to a low red car in silence, sliding quickly into the passenger seat, the violent slam of the door behind her making her jump. She watched him from beneath her lashes as he shot the car into the heavy traffic with a screeching of tyres, feeling rather frightened yet with a deep thrill of excitement coursing through her at the same time. Staring at the hard taut lines of his profile, she realised how much she had missed him since leaving Scotland.

He was driving very fast but not recklessly, his long-fingered brown hands totally in control of the powerful car. The tense silence built up, Laura's nerves stretching, her fingers restlessly twisting together in her lap. Tom's anger seemed tangible, filling the car as they shot out of London towards the coast.

She fumbled in her bag for her cigarettes. 'Dashboard.' The one sharply spoken word made her jump. She found the packet he was referring to.

'Do you want one?' she asked in a small breathless voice.

He nodded. 'Thank you.' Cold and polite.

She lit two, placing one between his lips, leaning near him. She could see the web of lines at the corner of his eye, the long dark eyelashes curling back from his eyelids, the smooth texture of his tanned skin, and her breath caught painfully as she retreated to her own corner of the car.

They drove on in silence until London was well behind them. Laura had no idea where they were, where they were going, gazing out of the window at the flat, rolling countryside, the sheep, the trees.

Finally Tom pulled the car to a halt. They were in

the middle of nowhere, totally alone, and she turned to stare at him in astonishment, wondering if he was mad.

'Why are we here?' she demanded. 'Where is here anyway?'

His grey eyes brooded on her face, but he seemed a little less angry now, more controlled.

'Whether you like it or not, we're going to talk.' His glance flicked the low horizon. 'And this is Kent.' She felt sure she heard mockery in his low voice.

'I really don't see what we have to talk about,' she said stiffly. How many times had she said that to him? she wondered.

'Let's start with you telling me why you didn't wait at the cottage as you promised, why you disappeared without leaving so much as a goddamned note, why you wouldn't speak to me on the phone, and finally why you've run away from your flat,' he suggested coolly, his face hard and cold, an expressionless mask.

He was leaning back, his arm along the back of her seat. Laura shifted uneasily, aware that she did not have to tell him anything. Strangely, though, she found that she wanted to, found herself searching for the right words.

'I . . . I came back to London without waiting, without telling you, because. . . .' She hesitated, savagely biting her lower lip, as she thought about her motives. 'Because I felt afraid to face you again after . . . after. . . .'

'After we'd made love?' he prompted, suddenly gentle.

Her face flamed. 'Y . . . yes. I was afraid you would look at me with contempt, see me as easy—just another woman who wanted you.' She broke off, unbearably embarrassed. She was making such a mess of this, but she did so want him to understand.

His fingers caught her chin and he tilted up her shy

violet eyes to his. 'And do you want me?' he demanded expressionlessly.

'Yes.' Her voice was barely above a whisper. It was useless to deny him, he already knew the truth.

Tom smiled, his grey eyes possessive, flaring with light. 'And how you hate to admit it,' he said, very softly. His hands moved upwards to cup her face, thumbs moving rhythmically against her fragile cheek-bones.

'Oh, Laura, I love you, you stubborn, infuriating child.' He shook his head wryly, the light gleaming in the vital darkness of his hair. 'I fell in love with you the moment I saw you in that restaurant with Grace, and you've been fighting me every inch of the way ever since.' His voice was deep, rough with emotion.

Laura stared at him, wide-eyed, incredulous. 'You love me?' she echoed dazedly. The grey eyes were dark, caressing.

'I love you,' he repeated slowly. 'And I've felt anger, jealousy, but never contempt, I certainly never thought you were easy, so you can stop thinking like that right now.' He lowered his head, his mouth touching hers, brushing her lips gently at first, then with a growing, deepening hunger that set her senses alight.

She responded unashamedly, passionately, pure need burning inside her. Tom loved her! How perfect, how beautiful, the only thing that mattered in her life.

Suddenly he put her away from him, his hands slightly unsteady as he lit two cigarettes. He stared into her face as he drew deeply on his cigarette. 'I want to tell you about my marriage,' he said flatly.

Laura frowned. 'You don't have to, I. . . .'

'I want to, I want you to know, because I'm sure you've heard the gossip and it's time to set things straight.' He stared straight ahead out of the windscreen his face hard and expressionless again. 'I met Julia when I was eighteen. She was twenty-five. We met in France—she lived there, and I was travelling through, sleeping rough, you know the sort of thing. I'd lived in that goddamned home for so long that I wanted, I burned to see the world, to prove that it really existed. She was beautiful, headstrong, wild and free.' He paused, his grey eyes searching Laura's, his voice flat and emotionless, totally devoid of feeling. 'I thought I loved her—oh, I know now that it was only infatuation, the love of an eighteen-year-old boy who knew nothing of the world, of love, but at the time I wanted her very badly. So I married her.'

Laura listened carefully as he spoke, her heart twisting with jealousy, thinking of, imagining him, young and strong and in love. His eyes told her that it had all been an illusion, but still it hurt her to know that he had loved so fiercely, that Julia had known that sweet love.

Tom raked a hand through the darkness of his hair. 'It was a disaster, of course, the biggest mistake of our lives. We were far too young, too immature. Julia was wild, totally, innocently selfish, spoiled and over-indulged by her parents, who were against the marriage right from the start.' The powerful shoulders lifted self-deprecatingly. 'And I—I guess I was just selfish, insisting that she married me, insisting that she lived up to my standards. Within a year she was pregnant with Luke and she hated it, hated the restrictions it put on her, hated what she considered the ugliness of her body and hated me for giving her the child. A year at that age makes a lot of difference, both of us had changed, matured, I guess. I found that the love I'd felt was gone, there was only pity, indifference.

'As soon as Luke was born Julia resumed her old life style, ignoring the child, ignoring me. There were horrific rows—we were deliberately cruel, destructive, Julia was blatently unfaithful and I was cold, almost brutal. I wish I could tell you that I tried to make it work, for Luke's sake, but I didn't. I was twenty years old, burning with anger, disappointment and resentment, and I thought it would be better for Luke to be brought up in reasonable peace, rather than in that brutal, bitter atmosphere. So I left, and as soon as I'd gone Julia perversely decided that she wanted me back, wanted to make a go of the marriage. She felt cheated, only wanted me because I wasn't available any more. Maybe I should have gone back, if only for Luke, but I couldn't—I didn't.' He finished in that same hard, remote voice.

Laura stared out of the window, watching two magpies swooping over the fields in graceful harmony, their bold colours catching her eye. Two for joy. Her heart was wrenched with pain at the terrible cruelty of it all.

'Why did you never divorce her?' she asked quietly, a question that had long haunted her.

Tom lit another cigarette. 'There seemed little point. I had no intention of marrying again and I was finished with love. And also I wanted some say in the way Luke was brought up. As her husband I was his legal guardian. Julia was using him in her fight against me. She would have fought for custody in a divorce case and she would have won, she would have ruined his life out of sheer spite, and apart from rights of access I would have been completely isolated from him. As it was, she only wanted money, and I could buy time with my son far more easily without a divorce,' he explained simply.

'I see,' Laura said sadly, still very shocked.

'No, you don't, my love.' The warmth in his voice turned her head towards him. He leaned forward and kissed her mouth very tenderly. 'The day after I met you I contacted my solicitors and instructed them to start divorce proceedings.'

'But. . . .'

'I didn't give a damn by that time, I only wanted to be free of her, and now . . . now it doesn't matter.' He kissed her again, his breath clean and cool against her lips. 'Marry me, Laura. You belong to me already, but I want you legally as well.' His eyes were possessive, dark with love.

She kissed his chin lovingly, hesitating. 'Tom, I don't want you to feel . . . well, I don't want you to feel that you have to marry me. I don't want to make any demands on you. I want you to be free, I want our love to be free. . . .' She did not finish, his mouth parted hers, warm, hungry and demanding, her words cut short.

'I'm committed to you already, little one, I'll always love you. Say you'll marry me,' he murmured persuasively against the side of her mouth.

'Yes,' she gave in, knowing a brilliant flaring of joy in her heart, her jealousy of Julia fading into nothing with the realisation that Tom did love her, would always love her. This time it was for ever, and all her old fears, her suspicion and mistrust, her coldness, dissolved away under the power of their love.

Tom smiled, a dark triumph glinting in his eyes. 'I thought I was in for another fight,' he teased her gently.

'I never fought you,' she smiled back at him provocatively.

The dark brows rose. 'No?'

'You were always angry,' she said sweetly.

'Sheer jealousy,' he admitted wryly, his fingers gently tracing the soft lines of her face. 'As soon as I saw you I wanted you, you were so shy, so beautiful.

The day I gave you a lift home from Grace's house—remember? I'd only called to ask her about you—I couldn't get you out of my mind for a second. I knew I couldn't rush you, though, that I'd have to wait until I had something to offer you. The illustration was the perfect way of getting to know you without frightening you off.'

'Oh, and I thought it was my talent with a brush that prompted you to offer me that commission,' said Laura, mock-angry.

'It was, partly. You're very talented. We work together perfectly—a good omen, yes?'

'Yes. Do carry on, I didn't mean to interrupt.' She wanted to hear him talking of his love for her, needed that reassurance.

'I didn't want to rush you, but every time you came near me I was burning up for you, and every time I touched you, although your response was so sweet, you flung the fact that I was married in my face. I was jealous of Premoli, of your kindness to him, God knows, I could have killed you both when I saw you in his arms, I was even jealous of my own son. I followed you to Scotland to find the two of you together, happy as larks. That's why I was cruel, I was beyond control, crazy for you. Forgive me?'

Laura kissed him, then said worriedly, 'I forgive you, of course I do. When I marry you . . . what about Luke? When he found us together . . . .!' Her voice trailed off as she remembered the expression on his young face.

'He was going through a very bad time—he knows how I feel about you. He'll get over it, he'll have to, I can't let you go,' Tom said raggedly. His arms tightened possessively around her. Laura could feel the fierce tension in his body and nestled closer.

'He said I looked like Julia,' she remembered sadly.

Tom shook his head. 'No, you're beautiful, truly beautiful. Tell me about Premoli.'

'There was never anything but friendship between us. He was comforting me that night at the party. I thought . . . I thought that Amanda was your lover.'

He was very surprised. 'Amanda? Yves would kill me if I laid a finger on her!'

'I know, it was very silly of me. She told me today about her husband, about them staying with you.'

'She's a good, astute friend. I've been hell to live with the past couple of days. When I got back to the cottage and you were gone I had to find you—I was crazy, you seemed to have disappeared without trace. I must remember to thank Amanda for bringing us together.' He was stroking his hand through her golden hair.

'Talking of thanks, I never did thank you properly for buying the silver casket for me. It's beautiful— thank you.' Laura touched her mouth to his, moving her lips against the firm warmth of his. His response was instant, demanding, his arms lifting her closer to his body.

'I love you, Tom,' she admitted drowsily, her hands touching his powerful shoulders slowly.

He lifted his head, the dark devouring intensity in his eyes making her heart stop beating. 'I've waited a lifetime for you, Laura—you'll never know how much I love you,' he murmured deeply.

'I'd like to,' she smiled at him, her eyes very tender, very beautiful.

He laughed exultantly, holding her tightly, gently tilting up her face to his.

He was about to show her, and they had all the time in the world.

A TRADITIONAL ITALIAN DISH

When Laura dines on Spaghetti Bolognese she is treating herself to a delicious and nourishing traditional pasta dish enjoyed by lovers of Italian food everywhere. Here's a simple recipe that will feed the whole family!

What you need:

1 large onion, chopped
2 cloves garlic, crushed (optional)
2 tbsp. olive oil
¼ cup carrot, diced
⅓ cup celery, diced
½ cup green pepper, diced
¼ lb. mushrooms, whole or chopped
½ lb. ground lean beef
¼ lb. ground veal
¼ lb. ground pork
1 cup dry red wine
1 tsp. oregano
¼ tsp. nutmeg
1 tsp. salt
½ tsp. freshly ground pepper
crushed and dried chilis to taste
2 cups canned tomatoes
5 oz. tomato paste
1 lb. pkg. spaghetti noodles
Parmesan cheese

What to do:

In a large pot, sauté onion and garlic in oil until onion is just transparent. Add carrot, celery, green pepper and mushrooms, and cook, stirring occasionally, on medium heat for two minutes. Add beef, veal and pork, crumble with a fork and brown lightly. Add wine and cook until evaporated. Add oregano, nutmeg, salt, pepper, chilis, tomatoes and tomato paste, turn heat to high and bring to a boil, stirring frequently. Turn heat down and simmer uncovered, stirring occasionally, for approximately 3 hours. Serve over spaghetti noodles, cooked as per package instructions. Sprinkle with Parmesan cheese.

Introducing...

Harlequin American Romance

An exciting new series of sensuous and emotional love stories—contemporary, engrossing and uniquely American. Long, satisfying novels of conflict and challenge, stories of modern men and women dealing with life and love in today's changing world.

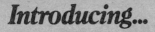

Available in May wherever paperback books are sold, or through Harlequin Reader Service:

In the U.S.
1440 South Priest Drive
Tempe, AZ 85281

In Canada
649 Ontario Street
Stratford, Ontario N5A 6W4

AR-1

Your FREE gift includes

Anne Mather—Born out of Love
Violet Winspear—Time of the Temptress
Charlotte Lamb—Man's World
Sally Wentworth—Say Hello to Yesterday